A TAROT PROPHECY AND OTHER STORIES

A Tarot Prophecy and Other Stories

STEPHEN TALLEVI

CONTENTS

To Sue and Isabel

First published by Stephen Tallevi 2024

First edition

CAPTURED SOULS

English Lake District, 1858

Lewis set the bouquet of Daffodils on her grave. Her tombstone lay towards the back of the churchyard, next to the old stone wall that enclosed the small cemetery of St. Bede. Engraved at the top of the tombstone were two hands clasped together—a testament to their everlasting love. Below the engraving, the epitaph read: *Harriet Parker. Her light will shine eternally. Requiescat In Pace.*

"Rest in peace, my love," he said tenderly, "When the time comes, we will walk hand-in-hand once more, as we used to."

It was just a few months ago that they had settled in the village of Elterwater, where he found employment as a bookkeeper at the gunpowder plant. Harriet was delighted when he told her the news. She loved the countryside and was eager to leave the crowded streets of London behind to begin a new life in Elterwater with him. They took up residence in a cozy cottage by a gentle stream, one of the many waterways that fed into the main river powering the factory. While he was away at work, she roamed the region in search of inspiration for her artwork, a series of landscape paintings commissioned by a dear friend of hers. It was during one of these outings that she came to discover the church at St. Bede.

The small church stood alone in a meadow along the western edge of the lake, two tall elm trees flanking the low stone wall surrounding both the church and its cemetery. A small wooden gate facing the rear of the church provided the only entrance into the church grounds. On the opposite shore of the lake, a series of imposing, craggy peaks towered above, dwarfing the church in comparison.

Beautiful beyond words, thought Harriet as she absorbed the subtle details of the scenery that lay before her, *this will be an absolute joy to paint.*

She went there almost every day, with her easel and pochade box in tow, painting the church and its surroundings for hours on end. On a singularly hot and humid afternoon, as Harriet was putting the final touches to her painting, a great thunderstorm caught her by surprise, forcing her to seek shelter under the canopy of one of the great elm trees. "Of all the rotten luck," she said out loud, as a clap of thunder broke overhead and a sudden gust of wind swayed the towering branches above her.

That evening Lewis arrived home to find a clergyman waiting for him outside his cottage gate.

"Reverend Anderson, what brings you here?" He glanced past the reverend to the closed door of the cottage. "Has Harriet not yet returned?"

Clearing his throat, the reverend replied in a subdued voice, "As you are probably aware, there was a violent storm this afternoon. Mrs. Parker was caught unawares and took shelter under an elm tree by the church yard. One of its large boughs broke free by the fierce wind, badly injuring your wife. By the time I found her, there was little I could do to save her. I'm so sorry, Mr. Parker."

Lewis stood in silence, then the meaning of the reverend's words took hold and he felt sick, his head spinning and his legs ready to give way. He swallowed hard and said unsteadily, "My...Harriet..."

The reverend nodded slowly. "You can take some solace in knowing that I had time to administer her last rights, Mr. Parker. Before her parting, she asked that I convey her final words to you—that she loves you, and that she wishes to be buried at St. Bede's cemetery. She passed away peacefully soon after communicating this to me."

Suddenly, the reverend reached out and caught Lewis by the arms before gently laying him down on the ground. The poor fellow had fainted.

Her tombstone cast its long shadow in the waning daylight. "It's time for me to go, Harriet, but I'll be back soon." He was about to leave but after a moment's reflection spoke to her once more. "By the way, I almost forgot to tell you, there are some lovely forget-me-nots growing next to the hedgerows we planted, a vibrant azure colour. I'll collect a bunch and bring them with me tomorrow. They will complement the daffodils quite nicely."

Reaching out, he placed his hand on her tombstone. He held it there for a minute before turning away and slowly heading towards the gate. This was the most difficult part of the day, leaving her all alone in the small graveyard. *Just ten minutes more*, he muttered to himself. *I can't face the thought of going back to an empty house just yet.*

He wandered among the tombstones, noting that most appeared quite old, the headstones stained green with the encroachment of moss over time. He read some of the dates as he walked past. *Seventeen-eighty-nine, seventeen—*

He suddenly paused and focused his attention on the epitaph beneath the date. Most of the words were too worn down to be read, while others were encrusted with fungal growth. But a few letters stood out clearly, as if recently scrubbed clean.

"H-e-l-p" he murmured. Below these, two more letters were visible; "m-e."

"Help me," he said in bewilderment. "How very queer." He scanned the epitaph carefully once more, but those were the sole decipherable letters. Hesitantly, he walked up to the tombstone. The engraving at the top featured a bible. *This must be a grave of a minister,* he thought. He tried to decipher the name. The first few letters read 'Brad'. He used his nail to scrape away at the dried moss that covered the remainder of the name. Small flakes of green fell away revealing the letters 'dock'.

"Braddock," he said in a slow, puzzled voice. "I'll ask Reverend Anderson about the name, perhaps Braddock was a clergyman at St. Bede. Uncanny about the message, though. Just a rare fluke I suppose, such events must occur sometimes. Still...I can't shake the feeling that there is something to this. Perhaps—"

He broke his train of thought to look up towards the gate. Darkness had settled in, and a sudden feeling of unease fell upon him as he fixed his gaze at what looked like the silhouette of a man.

"Reverend Anderson?" Lewis asked in a lowered voice.

There was no reply as the shadowy figure faded into the darkness.

The next afternoon, Lewis arrived at the cemetery to find Reverend Anderson standing by a grave, bending forward as he ran his fingers along the epitaph engraved on the tombstone.

Lewis studied him for a short while, then made his way to the tomb and greeted the reverend with a "Good afternoon."

The reverend straightened suddenly with a start.

"My dear fellow, you took me quite by surprise. I did not hear you approaching. But it is good to see you Mr. Parker. How have you been?"

"I am coping with my loss as well as can be expected," Lewis replied, redirecting the conversation before the reverend could inquire further, "Is that Braddock's tombstone you were looking at just now? I came across it last night and was curious if he had been a reverend at this church."

"Why yes, he was, but I know little about him. He was succeeded by a Reverend Clarke in 1779, who reached the ripe old age of eighty-seven by the time I arrived to replace him in 1834. If I recall correctly, he told me Reverend Braddock was responsible for creating this small cemetery. There was something else he mentioned about the cemetery...something about the number of graves...dear me, what was it..." He stroked his chin pensively. "Twenty-nine" he said suddenly. "There was never to be more than twenty-nine graves present. It's curious how that slipped my memory. I'm afraid your wife's grave brings the count to thirty, but I'm sure the good reverend will find it in his heart to forgive me, as I certainly could not refuse your wife's last wishes."

"No, you certainly could not," agreed Lewis. He then added;

"I noticed you were examining the epitaph quite closely when I arrived."

"Yes, I was. I thought I made out a word or two as I was walking by, but upon closer examination I realized that I was mistaken. The stone is heavily weathered, and moss encrusts much of the epitaph."

"Yes, I myself thought I could make out some words last night, but I can see now that I was mistaken as well. What was it you think you saw?"

With an uneasy laugh Reverend Anderson replied, "It's of no importance. But you seem to be most interested in our Reverend Braddock, Mr. Parker. We do have a few of his documents and his journal in our ecclesiastical archives, if you wish to examine them."

"I would, very much indeed."

"Then make your way over to the church once you are done here. You can join me for a cup of tea before looking over the documents."

The records of Reverend Braddock were few and did not reveal much about the man. It was only when Lewis reached the last few pages of the journal, recorded during the reverend's eighty-second year, that he stumbled upon a few curious facts.

The cemetery was established by the reverend after consultation with a German theologian by the name of Mr. Ubel. None of the particulars surrounding this individual are recorded—who he was, where he lived, or how the reverend came to meet the man. As to the reverend's interment, he requested that his sacred bottle of holy water be buried with him.

Next to this entry, scrawled along the page's border, was written *Absolvat me Deus.*

"My Latin is rusty but I'm fairly confident this translates to *May God forgive me*," murmured Lewis, then added after a moment's reflection, "But what are you asking forgiveness from, Reverend Braddock?"

His attention was drawn to a small piece of paper that protruded from behind the last page. He ran his finger along the inside binding. *Someone has torn out the final few pages,* he observed. *Who would do such a thing? Perhaps the pages held the answer to my question, one that was not meant to be shared...*

He returned the journal to the shelf. Next to it was that of Reverend Clarke. *Why not,* he said to himself as he removed the journal from the shelf, *I'm sure Reverend Anderson won't mind my taking a little while longer.*

Reverend Clarke's journal left Lewis with yet more unanswered questions. It was Reverend Clarke who decreed that St. Bede's cemetery should not exceed twenty-nine graves in number, and had the outer stone wall constructed so as to limit any possible expansion of the cemetery. *Why?* And why, on more than one occasion, had he sought the assistance of senior pastors from surrounding districts to help consecrate the grounds? As for more information on Reverend Braddock, there was little, just a single entry that referred to his predecessor as 'a poor, misguided soul.'

"Have you discovered any thing new about our Reverend Braddock?"

Lewis looked up from the journal and shook his head. "Unfortunately," he said as he got up to replace the journal, "nothing beyond what you shared with me earlier."

"We generally tend to live quiet, uneventful lives," added Reverend Anderson pleasantly.

"Tell me reverend, are there any surviving family members of Reverend Braddock?"

"I believe," he said after a moment's reflection, "a niece of his resides at Little Langdale. I don't recall her name, but I will find out for you. Mrs. Hill, my housekeeper, is a bit of a busybody. If anyone knows her name and where she resides, it will be her."

The name and address were duly acquired from Mrs. Hill, and a few days later Mr. Parker found himself in a modest parlor seated across from a pale, delicate old woman with silvery gray eyes that complemented the colour of her hair.

"Thank you for taking the time to see me, Mrs. Thatcher."

"Not at all, Mr. Parker. The reverend mentioned your interest in learning more about my late uncle, Reverend Braddock."

"Yes, I felt I ought to know a little more about the history of St. Bede's church, as my wife cherished the spot and is now laid to rest in its cemetery."

"Mrs. Hill told me about the terrible accident. Life can be so cruel at times. You have my condolences, Mr. Parker."

Lewis acknowledged her sentiment with a nod, but remained silent, prompting Mrs. Thatcher to continue;

"I did not know my late uncle very well. He mainly kept to himself and spoke little during family gatherings. I don't believe he was particularly well liked by his parish. As you may already know, he did establish the church cemetery, although Reverend Clarke's decree that it remain small, not more than twenty-nine graves I believe, was seen as unreasonable by many. So much vacant land surrounds the church."

"Yes, I can understand why people would see it that way. Tell me," Lewis continued, "did your uncle ever mention someone by the name of Mr. Ubel?"

"The name rings a bell...but I can't be certain." Mrs. Hill gave a small sigh as she shrugged her shoulders. "But I'm afraid, Mr. Parker, that I have little more to add. I wish I could have been of more help to you."

"You have been most helpful. Thank you again for your time."

He was about to get up from his seat when she added;

"Mr. Parker, before you go, there is one more thing. Behind you on the bookshelf you will find a bible. It belonged to my uncle. I'm not sure why he wanted me to have it—I'm not a religious person. I'd like to donate it to St. Bede's church. Do you mind leaving it with Reverend Anderson the next time you find yourself there? I feel that is where it should have remained all along."

"Not at all, Mrs. Thatcher. I'll see to it that he receives it this week."

That evening, seated at the kitchen table, Lewis examined the leather-bound bible with great care, leafing through its gilded pages one at a time, the flame of the candle flickering slightly with each page turn.

Admit it man, he said to himself in frustration, *there is nothing here. I felt certain the reverend would have written some notes within the bible, or perhaps concealed the missing pages from his diary. I know I did not hallucinate the 'Help Me' message that evening, and his own diary asks for mercy from God. But I remain totally in the dark as to how to help him.* Lewis buried his face in his hands and let out a sigh of exasperation. *Accept that this is a hopeless task. Give it up and retire for the night.*

He shut the book and in an uncharacteristic fit of anger slammed his fist down near the front edge of the bible. An image materialized ever so briefly within the fore edge of its gilded pages. Lewis stared at the bible in disbelief.

And then a moment's reflection reminded him of a book he had seen on display at the British Museum. The curator explained how a painted image on the exposed front edges of the book could only be seen when the pages were fanned out, forming a flat canvas. Fore-edge painting, he called it. The gilding of the pages, which is added after the image is painted, makes the painting impossible to see unless the pages are fanned.

"It's time to see your artwork, Reverend Braddock," Lewis said, somewhat hesitantly.

He picked up the bible by its sides, sliding his thumbs under the cover and his fingers above the back cover, so that he was grasping all the pages between its bindings. He then pressed the pages downwards with his thumbs, causing them to fan out. The image that materialized deeply unsettled him.

The scene was that of a cemetery at night. At the top of the image, tombstones could be seen. A cutaway view below portrayed the coffins buried underneath them. A series of tunnels connected each of the graves. A hunched figure in a black robe was next to one of the graves, a small, uncorked bottle in his hand. A ghostly white mist was rising from the coffin and streaming towards the opening of the bottle. There was the semblance of a face within the mist, one displaying great fear and sorrow.

My God, uttered Lewis, *what unspeakable evil have you perpetrated, Reverend Braddock?*

He let the bible fall onto the table as he leaned back in his chair, viewing the book with a sense of dread.

"Harriet," he said unsteadily under his breath as he rose suddenly from his seat, knocking over his chair, "This cannot be your fate!"

And with a sense of impending doom, he staggered out the door.

He stood for a moment outside the cemetery gate, catching his breath as he looked about uneasily. Long spectral shadows stretched out from the base of the tombstones, cast by the light of a full moon. *There is devilry in the air, I can feel it in my soul.* Quietly pushing the cemetery gate open, he made his way cautiously to Reverend Braddock's grave, the only sounds being the soft rustling of the elm leaves and his own footsteps.

He stood in silence before the tombstone, his heart filled with dread. With a tone of defiance, he finally spoke;

"What monstrous deed have you committed Reverend Braddock? How dare you ask for my help—"

Lewis suddenly fell silent, his attention drawn to a faint rustling noise. The sound of footsteps approaching.

"It is I who asked for your help, Mr. Parker."

Lewis turned to confront the man who spoke these words. Before him stood a tall, dark figure with piercing eyes set wide apart.

"Mr. Ubel," Lewis uttered with disgust.

"That is but one of my names, Mr. Parker. I have been given many over the centuries, as you may have already surmised." He took a step closer to Lewis and added in a darker tone, "I would advise you to listen carefully to what I have to say, if you truly care about the fate of your poor wife's soul."

Lewis stared into the bestial face before averting his gaze and giving a slight nod.

"Very wise of you, Mr. Parker. Let me begin by telling you a little about the reclusive Reverend Braddock. I have, as you can imagine, a talent for sniffing out morally vulnerable individuals, and our good reverend was certainly one. His innermost desire was to explore the delights the world had to offer, particularly those that would satisfy the carnal desires that were burning within him. And so, before his death, I made a bargain with him.

"I presented him with the opportunity to experience such a life, to live his years over again, to fulfill whatever depravity his small mind could imagine, and to do so freely, without the danger of being held to account by anyone, not even the law. The price of such unrestrained joy? Thirty souls, to be collected by him after his death by means of a unique bottle—a kind of spirit trap, that was to be interned with him. Once buried, I reanimated his corpse, where he spent his time tunneling his way to each new grave in order to capture its soul.

"A problem arose when, unbeknownst to me, the old fool decided to record our agreement in his journal, a most unwise decision as it was soon discovered and read by Reverend Clarke following Braddock's death. He took its contents very seriously, and so implemented measures to ensure the contract could not be fulfilled. The first of these was to limit the number of graves in the cemetery to twenty-nine. That is, until your wife was buried here. I now have my thirty souls, Mr. Parker."

"My God, you have...her soul?" Lewis stammered in a trembling voice.

"Not I, Mr. Parker, it still resides in the bottle held by the rotting corpse of Reverend

Braddock. You see, as a further precaution, Reverend Clarke had the cemetery blessed several times, believing it would free any of the captured souls. But in this regard he was mistaken. Instead, the consecrated soil hinders me from descending to retrieve my souls, while also preventing what remains of Reverend Braddock from ascending to the surface. This is why I need your assistance, and I am willing to trade your wife's soul for it."

Without hesitation, Lewis replied;

"What do you require of me?"

"I need you to get my collection of souls, Mr. Parker. Meet me on the other side of this wall. I have already excavated a six-foot hole next to it, but I cannot dig any further without hitting consecrated ground. Instead, you will use the spade to dig your way forward another foot, where you will connect to one of several tunnels leading to Reverend Braddock. Take the bottle from his hand. The moment you do so, I will release your wife's soul. Then bring the bottle back to me."

"Is the reverend...still—"

"He is not, Mr. Parker. He is a rotting corpse. He disregarded our pact of secrecy by recording our bargain in his journal. For this, I will enjoy tormenting his soul for a very long time..."

A damp, foul smelling air assaulted Lewis as he broke through to the connecting tunnel. He placed a handkerchief over his nose before peering into the darkness with the aid of a hurricane lamp. The ceiling of the tunnel was low, forcing him to proceed with his back steeply hunched forward. As he advanced, his breathing grew more laboured, compelling him to remove the handkerchief from his nose. The air was thin and stagnant, and soon the flame in his lamp began to flicker and dim, but not before he caught sight of a shadow just a few feet away. He staggered towards it, his head and back scrapping against the top of the tunnel as he found it impossible to maintain his hunched posture.

The shadow proved to be the opening to a grave. Lewis dropped to his knees and held the dim light above its bodily remains. He gave a start as he made out the ghastly grin of a skull.

"Dear God, please let this be the grave of Reverend Braddock," he uttered desperately.

The flame grew dimmer still, so that Lewis was forced to keep his face within inches of the corpse as he traced the light along the body towards its hands—a pair of skeletal remains which held...nothing. He hung his head in defeat, and whispered;

Forgive me my love, I have failed you. I do not have it in me to go forward, I can scarcely breathe...

The lamp slipped from his grasp and landed beside the corpse, its metal base striking an object. He bent closer to the ground as he ran his trembling hands around the lamp until they came upon a slight protrusion in the earth. Using his fingers, he unearthed a small glass bottle.

Suddenly, a faint light appeared before him, growing larger as he stared at its nebulous shape. As it grew brighter, he could discern the outline of a face, then its features. Loving, caring eyes stared at him.

"Harriet, my God...it's really you," he stammered as he gasped for air. "I have little time. Together...soon." Turning, he headed to the entrance of the cave.

Lewis stumbled out of the tunnel and fell upon his knees, struggling for air. "Give it here, quickly!" demanded the beast, leaning down into the hole to snatch the bottle from Lewis' outstretched arm. He held the bottle to his ear, listening for a moment before a wide, ghastly grin spread across his face.

"You have done well, Mr. Parker. Let me assist you as you make your way out." He extended his hand towards Lewis, who did not accept it.

"I see...very well, have it your way."

Lewis turned and headed back into the tunnel, as the dug earth collapsed back into the hole to seal its entrance. He was soon crawling forward on his hands and knees, too weak to walk. The flame of the lantern gave a final flicker then died. He couldn't go on. He sat himself up against the tunnel wall, his breathing coming in short, shallow breaths.

"Harriet," he whispered.

She was there suddenly, her radiant spirit floating next to him, her loving face looking directly at him. Her eyes expressed bewilderment.

"Come now," he said lovingly, "you didn't think for a moment that I would leave you all alone down here, did you?"

Smiling, he held out his hand, and when he felt the warmth of her soul upon it, he shut his eyes and took his last breath.

WOLF HUNT

Niagara, Canada, 1910

"**B**lasted nuisance this snow," said Edward in his gruff voice, watching the large snowflakes descend from the sky through the French doors of the drawing room. "I'm all for a white Christmas, but this really is too much. It's been snowing steadily for two days now. Can't imagine any of my other guests making the trek from Queenston. These country lanes won't be cleared for a few days yet." He turned and made his way to the fireplace, taking a seat next to his old friend Colonel Callington.

"Another scotch for you, Colonel? So glad you had the good sense to arrive a couple of days earlier."

"No thank you, Edward, think I'll relax with my pipe. I'm pretty sharp when it comes to reading the weather. Experience you know, as it could make the difference between life and death on the battlefield."

"Quite so," agreed Edward.

The Colonel took a few puffs of his pipe before adding; "Fortunate that your niece has been staying with you these past few weeks. Edith is always such good company. She'll make Christmas feel more festive, even if it is just the three of us. A very considerate girl. Surprised she hasn't married yet."

"Needs to settle down," grumbled Edward. "Always traveling about, never staying in one spot long enough for any man to take serious notice of her."

"Wasn't your nephew Marrock to attend as well? He must be in his mid-twenties by now. Haven't seen him since he was a young lad."

"Had to send him abroad to boarding school. The shock of what happened was too great for him."

"Bad business that," admitted the Colonel.

"But he's turned out just fine. Came back to Canada last year. Got himself a good job as a law clerk with Fraser & Williams while he continues his studies in law. I wouldn't be the least surprised if he rose to a partnership at the firm within a few years of getting his degree. A damn shame he won't be able to make it for Christmas."

The Colonel nodded his head in agreement. He noted the time on the mantel clock as he tapped the ash from his pipe. "We still have a couple of hours before dinner," he said as he rose from his chair, "How about a game of snooker?"

"Splendid idea. Our usual wager?"

"A most delicious meal, Edward," commented Colonel Callington, "You really do have the most wonderful cook."

"I second the Colonel's opinion," added Edith. "I've been thoroughly spoiled these past few weeks. I may just have to convince Mary to come with me when I leave."

Edward chuckled. "You will do no such thing. Mary has been with me for twenty-five years. As fond as she is of you, she would never leave. What you need is to settle down and get married."

"Oh dear uncle, let's not start that conversation again. One day I shall probably settle down, but for now I'm enjoying my travels as an independent woman far too much."

"Stubbornly independent," murmured Edward as he raised the glass of port to his lips.

"I heard that, uncle," said Edith with a smile. "You should know—" Her conversation was interrupted by the ringing of the front doorbell.

"Who on earth could it be at this hour on Christmas Eve?" inquired Edward. "And where could they possibly have come from in this weather?" His voice carried a touch of apprehension.

Suddenly, the doors to the dining room swung open. Arthur, the manservant, looking pale and short of breath, stepped forward and said, "Master Edward, please come quickly, sir, it's your nephew, Mr. Wood—he's in a bad way."

"Marrock!" Edward burst out as he rose from his seat and rushed out of the room, the others following close behind.

Marrock was sitting near the doorway where he had collapsed upon entering. The housekeeper had sensibly fetched a blanket from the study to wrap around his shivering form.

"Step aside, and let me have a look at him," commanded the Colonel. He tossed the blanket aside and after a few quick observations said, "Heartbeat is strong, skin is cold but he's not pale. A slight shiver but we'll soon take care of that. Let's get him in front of a fire and get some Brandy into him."

The Colonel and Edward lifted Marrock to his feet. Each taking an arm over one of their shoulders, they lead him to the drawing room and sat him next to the fireplace where Arthur had stoked a blazing fire. Ten minutes later, Marrock had stopped shivering and was leaning forward in his chair and rubbing his hands towards the flames.

"That's my lad," said Edward, relieved to see his nephew recovering so quickly from the cold. "Now get that Brandy inside you before you tell us how in blazes you managed to make your way here on foot."

Edward took a few sips and felt a surge of warmth fill his body. "That hit the spot," he said appreciatively as he handed the glass back to Arthur. "I daresay it was a damn foolish thing for me to do, but I was not going to miss my first Christmas with you in fifteen years, so I set off with my automobile immediately after lunch and made my way here. Thought they would have cleared most of the roads by then, but clearly, I was greatly mistaken. About two miles distance from here, the auto failed to make it up a slight curving grade and before I knew it I was sliding backwards and straight into a snowbank. I had no option but to leave the auto there. Grabbed my valise from the trunk and started walking. No fear of getting lost as I could see the lights from the manor quite clearly. I nearly froze getting here, but I felt confident I'd make it."

"You're fortunate you didn't encounter any wolves along the way," Edward pointed out. "There have been more of them than usual this winter. I suspect the cold and snow has driven them here in search of food. But you're here safe and sound, that's all that matters. You'll join us for dinner of course, once you have had the opportunity to change into some warm clothes—"

"My valise!" exclaimed Marrock.

"Arthur will see to it. You dropped it just outside the front door. You'll find it in the guest room he's prepared for you. But before you head upstairs, let me properly introduce you to our guests, both of whom you've met when you were a young lad of eight."

"I remember you both," remarked Marrock as he rose from his seat and offered his hand to Colonel Callington. "This is twice you've rescued me Colonel, once from my mother's cottage and now from freezing to death at uncle's doorstep."

"Nonsense my boy, you were never in any real danger. Glad to see you looking so fit and doing well for yourself. Earlier this evening your uncle was telling me about your post with Fraser & Williams."

"Thank you, Colonel. I'm enjoying my work with the firm. They keep me busy, but not to the extent that I can't carry on with my studies. I hope to be called to the bar in two years time."

"That would be an admirable accomplishment," said the Colonel encouragingly.

Marrock nodded his head appreciatively before turning to face Edith. Smiling, he said;

"And I recall our short time together as children, Cousin Edith. We spent an afternoon playing in uncle's garden, imagining ourselves to be great explorers."

"That's right," Edith replied slowly, recalling the memory. "I had nearly forgotten. That's probably how I got my desire to travel. So you see uncle, you can blame Cousin Marrock for my gypsy lifestyle."

"Guilty as charged," replied Marrock with a chuckle. "But it's time I went upstairs and changed. I've kept all of you away from your dinner for far too long. I will join you in a few minutes."

Dinner proved to be a genial affair, with much of the conversation focused on Edith and her travels. Marrock was most interested in her visit to Romania and the superstitions she encountered there. There was a lively debate among the group about the existence of vampires and werewolves, with Colonel Callington being adamant that such creatures could not exist, although he grudgingly admitted that he had witnessed some queer events when he was stationed in India, so perhaps stranger things could occur elsewhere. "After all, England has its fair share of ghosts," he concluded.

The hours after dinner passed pleasantly with a game of bridge. The final round ended by half-past midnight, after which Marrock was the first to bid everyone goodnight and retire to his room. Edith followed shortly thereafter, while Edward and the Colonel made their way to the study for a nightcap.

The group gathered the next morning for a late breakfast of bacon, eggs, toast and haddock. Once seated, Edward asked; "I trust everyone had a good night's sleep?"

"Hardly," growled the Colonel. "Blasted wolves howled all night long. I had half a mind to fetch my hunting riffle to silence the creatures from my bedroom window."

"Yes, I heard them as well," added Marrock. "Tell me Colonel, have you hunted wolves before?"

"Occasionally I set traps and hunt them when they encroach on private property. I'll never forget a monster of a beast your uncle and I killed nearby the day I...that is...some fifteen years previous during a particularly harsh winter. We had laid down some traps near the woods and were heading back to the manor when a great howl ripped through the stillness of the morning. I spun around and saw a great white wolf with one of its paws caught in our trap. We each fired our riffles from thirty yards out and one of our bullets hit the creature. To this day we don't know whose bullet proved lethal, but the beast dropped dead like a stone," he added proudly.

"Magnificent beast," put in Edward. "I have its head mounted in my study, next to the cheetah I bagged in Africa. You should have a look at it later, I'm sure you'll be impressed."

"I'm sure I will," Marrock replied.

"On a more pleasant note," said Edith, "I think I'll go to the stables after breakfast and check on the horses. I was hoping to ride Jasmine this weekend, but the snow is too deep."

"Get one of the stablehands to escort you," demanded Edward.

"That's alright, uncle, I can manage quite well on my own."

"So you keep reminding me," Edward said under his breath. "And what are your plans for this afternoon, Marrock?"

"If you don't mind, uncle, I'll go to my room and see if I can't get some sleep before tea. Like the Colonel, the wolves kept me up most of the night. I heard the clock strike five before I nodded off."

"By all means, my boy. The Colonel and I will be playing snooker, should you wish to join us after your rest."

"Thank you, I think I will."

Marrock joined the two men in the billiards room sometime later. They played for a few hours before heading to the drawing room for afternoon tea. The Colonel emerged victorious in all games except one.

"How are the horses?" asked Edward after having sipped his Darjeeling tea.

"They seemed content," replied Edith as she studied the assortment of finger sandwiches before selecting one with beef tongue. "I gave Jasmine a good grooming. I didn't feed the horses as I presumed the stablehand would being doing so later today."

"Five-thirty is his usual time, which means he's probably there now."

A short while later Arthur discretely entered the room and made his way over to Edward, leaning in to whisper something in his ear.

"Good God!" Edward cried under his breath, the colour draining from his face.

"What is it uncle?" Marrock asked in alarm.

"Nettle...my prize horse...killed by a wolf," he stammered.

"But that's simply not possible, uncle," said Edith in disbelief. "I barred the stable doors after I left earlier this afternoon. There is no possible means by which a wolf could have made his way in."

They were huddled around the entrance of the first stall. Ben, the stablehand, was standing within, holding an oil lamp a few feet above the horses' head, illuminating the savage wounds across its throat, the surrounding straw saturated with blood.

"Poor Nettle," Edward said with solemnity, "such a brutal way to die."

"Indeed, it is," agreed the Colonel. "But it's a very singular thing," he continued after a moment's pause, "that none of his flesh has been eaten. Surely the wolf killed because it was hungry, yet there are no signs of any part of Nettle having been consumed. It's also fortunate Jasmine wasn't attacked."

"That is curious," Marrock said slowly. Addressing Ben, he asked; "You say that the wooden bar that locks the outer door was knocked off the supporting pegs. Its a heavy piece of wood. I don't see how a wolf could accomplish that."

"I don't know, sir. As you probably noticed there are plenty of wolf tracks all around the stable. Perhaps a constant attack on the doors could have dislodged the beam. It would have been easy enough to enter the stable after that."

"Yes, that's a possibility," mused Marrock. The group lapsed into an uncomfortable silence as they pondered the unlikely explanation, unable to come up with any alternative. It was Edward who broke the silence.

"Let's get Nettle away from here, Ben. Get the stable boys to help. The three of us will also give a hand. Let's move the carcass to the abandoned woodshed. Then have the boys scrub down the stall and lay down new hay. I'll have Edith come out to feed and groom Jasmine once the smell of blood is gone. Hopefully that will calm the horse for the remainder of the evening."

Dinner was a quiet affair that evening. After the dessert course, Colonel Callington suggested to Edward and Marrock that they retire to the library.

"I'm coming as well," Edith said briskly. "This affair has disturbed me a great deal and if you are going to discuss it further then I have every right to be present."

"Of course, Edith," agreed Edward. "Then there's no need to move ourselves to the library, we can discuss matters here. I trust you don't object to my smoking a cigar."

"Not at all. And please feel free to smoke your pipe as well, Colonel."

The Colonel smiled and nodded his head in reply. Sitting back in his chair for a moment's reflection, he lit his pipe and took a few puffs before stating;

"I daresay the loss of Nettle under such savage circumstances puts a damper on our Christmas spirit, but we must take action if we are to prevent any further occurrences. Now that the wolves have tasted blood, they will be bolder and come closer to the house. It will not be safe for ourselves or any of the servants to be outdoors."

"That also holds true for any guests that may yet decide to visit us in the next few days," put in Edward.

"As such, the only solution is to do away with the beasts," concluded the Colonel.

"But surely we cannot kill all the wolves?" asked Marrock incredulously.

"No need to," replied the Colonel, taking another puff of his pipe. "We only need to kill the dominant male of the pack and the rest will disband and leave the area. I propose that I set out traps tomorrow morning. It has stopped snowing, so I can trace their tracks and hide the traps nearby."

"Should I come with you?" inquired Edward.

"No need, I can handle it on my own. Don't expect it will take more than a couple of hours. I'll take an early breakfast and be on my way by eight o'clock. Perhaps you can ask Ben to grease the traps tonight and store them in the trap sack. I'll need a hunting rifle as well."

"Certainly, I'll have Arthur convey the message," replied Edward as he got up to ring the servant bell.

"Thank you, Edward. And now that that's settled, may I suggest we play a round of bridge to distract ourselves from tonight's regrettable occurrence? Your niece and nephew proved to be formidable foes last night, and I would appreciate the opportunity to challenge them again."

Refreshing to see the sun again and to take in the crisp morning air, thought the Colonel as he headed towards the woods some hundred yards north of the manor. The snow was a foot deep but soft and powdery so that he could easily make his way through it. *Shouldn't take me more than an hour to set the traps. Not as quick as I used to be, but I'm still in pretty good shape for a man of fifty, unlike Edward, who despite being a few years younger has acquired a rotund figure. I really must have a talk with him about his eating habits.*

He discovered the wolf tracks soon after entering the woods, meandering their way around the pine trees, sometimes doubling back on themselves. "Curious behaviour," he murmured, "nevertheless, best if I lay the traps along this section as it displays plenty of activity. One of the animals is a good deal larger than the others judging by this set of prints. Probably the dominant male. Hopefully it will be his paw caught in one of the traps when I return later today."

Along a thirty yard stretch the Colonel set six traps, covered them over with snow, then sprinkled extract of fish oil around each, the scent acting as a lure. "That should—"

He stopped in mid-sentence as he caught sight of a large shadow moving among the trees. Sliding the rifle off his shoulder, he carefully made his way forward. After a few yards, he became aware of additional movement on either side of him. *This wolf pack must be larger than I anticipated,* he reasoned. *I get the sense that the brutes are trying to surround me—this won't do. Time to make my way back.*

Carefully retracing his steps, he had not traveled more than a dozen yards when suddenly he cried out in agony. The steel teeth of a trap had driven through the toe of his boot and deep into his flesh. He cursed as he fell to one knee to brush the snow away from the trap.

How the blazes did this get here? It can't be one of mine!

He looked around uneasily as he tightened his grip on the riffle. He could now make out the large timber wolves staring at him from between the trees, motionless, as if waiting for something to happen. The sudden silence was deafening.

Get a grip man—focus on getting your foot out of this trap.

Placing his hands on each side of the trap, he pressed down firmly on the release levers. The pain was excruciating but he managed to pry his foot free from the clutches of the iron teeth. Warm blood rushed out from the wound, soaking his thick woolen sock. Using the rifle as a crutch, he struggled to his feet. It was then that he heard the approaching gallop of a large beast.

"Where the blazes is everyone?" asked Edward in an agitated voice. It was ten-thirty and no one was seated at the breakfast table. Marrock entered the dining room a minute later and, noticing the expression on his uncle's face, asked, "What's the matter, uncle? You seem worried this morning."

"I am. For starters, where's Edith?"

Marrock shrugged his shoulders. "I have no idea."

"Ring Arthur. Let's hope he knows."

"Your niece has just returned from the stables, sir," explained Arthur a few moments later. "She went to groom Jasmine this morning at about half-past nine, sir."

"I see," replied Edward, having calmed down by the news. "And I presume the Colonel has returned by now," he added as he took his seat at the head of the table.

"Not that I'm aware of, sir."

"What? Still not back? He's been gone over two-and-a-half hours. Must be doing a pretty thorough job of it. Still, it's most unlike the Colonel to take so long for such a straightforward task. I don't like it. Tell Ben to meet me at the front door, I think I'll go and check on the Colonel."

"Do you mind if I join you, uncle?"

"Not at all, my boy. I was hoping you'd ask."

"I'm coming as well." Edith had been standing at the doorway long enough to catch the last few sentences of Edward's conversation. She looked anxious, her cheeks flushed by being out in the cold. "My nursing background could prove helpful if the Colonel is hurt."

Edward reflected a moment. "Yes...an injury would explain his delay in getting back." He got up from his seat and said abruptly; "Arthur, tell Ben to bring the toboggan with us. If memory serves me correctly, it is still propped up against the woodshed. We can use it as a stretcher should the Colonel be injured."

They followed the Colonel's tracks to his body. He was lying face down in the snow, the spine below his skull protruding where a set of massive jaws snapped it in two.

"God almighty," murmured Edward, "what manner of beast did this?"

"There are only wolf tracks here," Marrock observed. "It must have been a formidable beast to snap his spine like that."

"Horrible," murmured Edith. "Such savagery."

Edward picked up the rifle next to the body and examined it. "He didn't even get a chance to fire a shot."

Marrock noticed a red hue on the snow around one of the Colonel's boots. He bent down and lifted it by the heel. Blood dripped from the toe cap.

"His own foot was caught in a trap," Marrock pointed out, before letting it drop back onto the snow.

"The Colonel would never be so careless," Edward said after a moment. "I don't know what happened here, but something is amiss. Let's get his body back to the house. We'll need to keep it in the cold for the time being. I think we have little choice but to lock it up in the woodshed with Nettle's carcass. I pray the roads will be cleared by tomorrow so we can go for help."

Marrock and Ben lifted the body onto the toboggan. Edward insisted on pulling the sled back to the manor. It was all he could do for his old friend.

That evening, Marrock asked if he could speak to Edward privately in the study.

"Certainly. But I hope you haven't decided on leaving tomorrow."

"Not at all. What I wish to discuss is the Colonel's death. I'm certain I know what happened in the woods this morning."

Edward raised his eyebrows in surprise and looked at him in silence for a moment before motioning Marrock towards the study. The two men sat across from each other next to the glowing embers of the fireplace.

"As incredulous as this may sound," Marrock began, "we need to go back to the events of fifteen years ago, when I was only a boy of eight, in order to understand the circumstances surrounding the Colonel's death. Father had died a few years earlier in a hunting accident, after which you allowed mother and I to stay in the small cottage located at the forest's edge. I didn't understand why we couldn't continue to live here until weeks later when mother told me that you strongly disapproved of your brother's marriage to her. You saw her as nothing more than an attractive yet poor Romanian peasant unworthy of your brother's hand in marriage. You wanted little to do with her...or me."

"Come now, that's not fair, I—"

Marrock held up his hand.

"Let me finish, uncle. Mother and I were forced to fend for ourselves in the months that followed. That winter proved especially harsh and our food reserves dwindled to the point where mother had no choice but to look to you for help. Late one morning, she left the cottage and made her way to the manor. She never arrived. Everyone believed she had simply abandoned me, unable to care for her son as a single mother."

"That is precisely what occurred," confirmed Edward. "The Colonel was visiting that week and decided to check in on you and your mother. He found you alone sitting at the kitchen table, half-starved and nearly frozen to death."

"True, mother had been gone for three days by the time the Colonel arrived. But let me continue as I assure you everything will make sense shortly."

Marrock leaned forward in his chair. Edward noticed there was a different look about his face. His pupils were full and reflected the light from the glowing embers with a certain intensity.

"You see," continued Marrock, "mother never arrived at the house because she stepped into a trap and was shot dead moments later."

"My poor lad," exclaimed Edward, "you are confusing our killing of the great wolf with the cowardly disappearance of your mother."

"I am not," came the quiet response. "The two events are one and the same."

At that moment, Edward was looking directly over Marrock's shoulder to the mounted wolf head. Slowly, he shifted his eyes away from the trophy and turned his attention back to his nephew.

"You're not mistaken, uncle, I have the same eyes as your wolf trophy, for you see, she was my mother."

He has lost his mind, thought Edward, and yet the phrase chilled his blood.

"The knowledge that mother was special, one who possessed the ability to take on the form of a beast—a 'shapeshifter'—was known only by me. That fateful day she transformed into her inner beast, a great wolf, as it was the only way she could reach your place under such frigid weather. I watched from our window as she made her way to the edge of the woods where she let out a dreadful howl. A moment later I heard a gun shot and watched in horror as she collapsed to the ground. I was in such a state of shock that all I could do was stand there, trembling with fear. And then two men—you and the Colonel—approached from the direction of the manor and took her away. Eventually, I made my way to the kitchen and sat down at the table, where I was content to die. But three days later the Colonel arrived and brought me here, where you soon sent me abroad to boarding school."

"You're...delusional," stammered Edward.

Marrock ignored the remark and continued.

"The Colonel's story during my first evening here confirmed that it was the two of you who killed her. I came to this room later that evening and saw my mother for the first time in fifteen years, as a decapitated head on a wall. How could anyone inflict such cruelty on such a beautiful creature, I asked myself. And I knew then that I had to inflict the same punishment on the two of you. It was a simple enough plan. I savagely tore Nettle's throat knowing the Colonel would go and set traps for the wolves the next morning. I got there earlier and waited, placing a trap in his path when the opportunity presented itself, later snapping his spine in two as he struggled to his feet after freeing his foot from my trap."

A look of fear appeared in Edward's eyes as he uttered the words; "You're mad."

"Unfortunately for you, uncle, I am not. You see, I inherited mother's special gift." Marrock drew his snarling lips back, revealing sharp canine teeth that lined the long snapping jaws emerging from his open mouth.

The timber wolves had gathered outside the French doors of the study. Marrock swung them open. They stared at him expectantly. He stepped aside, as they headed towards Edward's decapitated body to feast.

MASKED GODS

New York, 1958

Over the last six years, my days have typically started following the death of stranger. Man, woman or child, it makes no difference to my routine. I start by washing the corpse before flexing the limbs to relieve the stiffness caused by rigor mortis. Sometimes I end up breaking or dislocating bones or tearing the skin. Embalming is not a gentle process.

Today, I begin my work on a male individual in his twenties. I do not know how he died, but his face reflects a sense of tranquility. The body is in excellent condition, not even a blemish on the face. And what an exceptional face it is. Full lips, chiseled jaw, a Greek nose. *The face of a god.*

I make an incision near the back of the neck to expose a major artery and the jugular vein, both of which I slit as well. I connect the hose from the embalming machine to the artery and attach a tube to the jugular vein so that the blood can drain out while the embalming fluid is pumped into the body. The process takes a couple of hours, after which time I begin my work on the face.

I fill out the sunken cheeks with some cotton and insert serrated eye-caps beneath the eyelids so that they stay shut. As a last step, I fix wires into the upper and lower jaws, twisting them together so that the mouth remains closed. Taking a step back, I look at my finished work with a critical eye.

Flawless. Absolute perfection. Such beauty in death, and it is now up to me to capture it. It will be a slow process, but the end result will do *Apollo* proud.

The skies had cleared by the time Alan left the funeral home that afternoon. The sun was warm and bright, and the scent of rain was still in the air. He took a few deep breaths before massaging the back of his stiff neck.

That was a long session, he thought to himself, *but the end result was well worth it.*

He looked down at the black briefcase he was carrying and slowly nodded his head in approval. "Yes," he murmured, "it was well worth the effort."

When he got to the bus stop he removed his rain jacket, lit a cigarette, and made up his mind to walk home instead. *Unusually warm day for this time of year. Might as well take advantage of it. Fresh air will do me good.*

The barking of a dog caught his attention as he walked along Woodside Avenue. There was a small park across the road where some children were chasing a terrier that had evidently stolen their ball. He stopped to light another cigarette before lazily looking over the area. His attention was drawn to a young woman sitting on a bench. She was looking down with a pensive frown at a partially unfolded map, biting softly on her lower lip.

I can't believe my eyes, Alan said to himself as he tossed the cigarette aside. *She is the spitting image...a radiant round face, a perfectly straight nose, full round lips, and wavy, long blond hair. I must get a better look.*

He straightened his tie as he quickly made his way across the street towards the park bench.

"Excuse me, ma'am," he said in a friendly tone. The woman looked up in surprise.

"I'm sorry if I startled you. I was just walking by and couldn't help but notice that you appeared lost." He nodded towards the map resting on her lap. "Perhaps I can point you in the right direction."

"Why, that's very kind of you, Mr...?" Her blue eyes looked at him inquiringly.

"Brown, Alan Brown. And it's no trouble at all. I've lived in Queens most of my life. Know the area quite well."

"Thank you, Mr. Brown. I must admit, I could use some help right about now."

"Don't mention it. Now, where is it you're heading?"

"I'm trying to make my way to 58th Street and 39th Avenue. I got off the bus a few stops back. The driver said he didn't go as far as 58th Street. I'd been walking for twenty minutes before I realized I was lost."

"The good news is that you're not far from where you want to go," Alan put in encouragingly. "58th and 39th, you say. There's a school close by, a Saint Anthony Academy that—"

"That's where I'm headed!" she exclaimed.

"You don't say. My niece and nephew attend classes there. I occasionally drive them to school when their mother has to leave early for work. Are you a teacher?"

"Yes, I'll be starting in a couple of weeks. I'm taking over for someone who is retiring."

"That's great, I'm sure you'll like it there. Everyone is real friendly." He reached into the pocket of his raincoat and took out a packet of cigarettes, offering her one.

"No thank you, I don't smoke."

He took one for himself as he said casually; "If you feel up to it, we can walk there. It's not more than 15 minutes from here. You're not likely to flag down a cab in this neighbourhood so early in the afternoon. Naturally I'll carry your suitcase for you."

"Oh no, I couldn't ask that of you. I can manage. I travel light."

"It's no trouble at all, I assure you," Alan said with a smile as he reached for her luggage.

"Then it's only fair that I carry your briefcase."

His grip inadvertently tightened around the handle. "That's kind of you to offer, but it's no problem for me to carry both."

As they walked along the street, he did his best to answer her many questions about living in Queens. When they turned north onto 58th Street, Alan inquired;

"If you don't mind me asking, where are you from?"

"Connecticut. The teacher I'm replacing, Mrs. Miller, was also from there. She was a close friend of my parents, so naturally was aware of my occupation as a teacher. When the time came to retire, she reached out to me and said she could arrange for me to have her position. So here I am."

"And here," added Alan, placing her luggage down next to the steps that led up to the front entrance, "is the school."

"Thank you so much, Mr. Brown. You have been so kind."

"Don't mention it. By the way, I'd love to tell my niece and nephew that I met the new teacher at their school, that is, if you're OK with letting me know your name."

"How inconsiderate of me!" she cried out, her checks reddening slightly. "I'm Mary, Mary Anderson."

"It was a pleasure walking with you, Miss Anderson. Say..." Alan hesitated slightly before continuing, "would it be alright if I left you my phone number? Perhaps you could give me a call once you've settled in and let me know how you're doing. It would be swell to hear from you."

"Of course. That's very thoughtful of you, Mr. Brown."

"Please, call me Alan." He removed a pen from his shirt pocket before rummaging through the pockets of his rain jacket in search of something to write on.

"Here, use this." Mary removed the map from her purse and offered it to him. He jotted his name and number along the border and handed it back, and with a tip of his hat said; "Good day, Miss Anderson."

Mary nodded her head and smiled in reply.

When she reached the top of the steps she turned and watched as he made his way down the street. *Such a nice man, a charming smile and quite attractive too,* she told herself. *I'd place his age at around thirty. And no wedding band...*

She stepped into the school, already having made up her mind to call him in a few weeks' time.

Once home, Alan hurried down the steps to the sparsely furnished basement and made his way to a locked door at the far end. Unlocking it, he entered the dark interior of a small room and ran his hand along the wall until he located the light switch. A series of overhead lights flickered to life, illuminating his prized collection neatly aligned along the far wall. Carefully removing the object from his briefcase, he hung it with the others.

"That makes five," he said proudly. "One more and my collection will be complete."

Mary called a couple of weeks later. She explained that she was staying with Mrs. Miller until she could find accommodations of her own. Alan offered to help her find a place as he had some free time and could go and see a few rentals on her behalf. Perhaps they could meet the following week at a coffee shop so he could review his findings with her. She gladly accepted his invitation.

"The apartment on 65th Place looks wonderful, and the rent is reasonable for such a lovely unit," gushed Mary.

"I thought you'd like it. It's nice and bright too, the large living room window faces east. The landlady assured me the tenants on either side are quiet."

Mary looked at him with tenderness in her eyes. "Thank you, Alan, you've been very kind."

"Think nothing of it, glad I could be of help." Changing the subject, he asked; "So, Mary, what did you do prior to becoming a teacher?"

"Not much, I'm afraid. I went to a teacher's college right after high school and then spent a few years as a teaching assistant before getting this job."

"What did you do during your summers?"

"I went hunting."

Alan raised his eyebrows in surprise.

She laughed and said, "That's the reaction I get from most people. You see," she went on after taking a sip of her coffee, "mother was very ill for quite some time, and had to spend six months a year at a sanatorium. During the summers, my father had no idea what to do with me, so he took me on his hunting excursions. We had a cabin of our own, so we'd stay out for weeks at a time."

"What did you hunt?" Alan asked curiously.

"Primarily small game, but father did occasionally hunt deer as well. I got pretty good at preparing the meals. I remember one day he placed a rabbit on the counter and showed me how to skin and butcher it. I almost passed out!"

"But you didn't," Alan volunteered.

"You are correct. In fact, I became very proficient at it, 'frighteningly so,' father would say." She leaned forward and cupped her hands around the coffee mug before continuing; "Both my parents have passed away, so there was nothing to keep me in Connecticut. When this job offer arrived, I jumped at the opportunity. But enough of about me. I'd love to know more about you, Alan. You haven't yet told me what you do for a living."

Alan cleared his throat. "Well," he began somewhat nervously, "I hope this doesn't disturb you, as it invariably does most people I tell, but I'm an embalmer for funeral homes."

"It doesn't disturb me in the least," Mary replied reassuringly. "In fact, I think it's quite a noble profession, ensuring folks remember their dearly departed as the beautiful people they once were, now resting peacefully in their coffin."

Alan was speechless for a moment before he said with much relief; "Boy, am I glad you feel that way!"

Mary moved into her new apartment a few weeks later. Their meetings became more frequent and included dining out as well as the movies. At times, she could detect a hint of admiration in his eyes when he looked at her, but he did not give any signs of wanting to take the friendship to a more intimate level. Then, quite unexpectedly, while driving her home after a movie, he said;

"I'm going on a fishing trip this weekend with a few of my friends, something we do every year at this time. I was wondering if you would be willing to house sit while I was gone. It would be a good way for you to familiarize yourself with the place, as I'm hoping you'll feel comfortable enough to start visiting me."

"Oh Alan, of course I will," she said softly.

He smiled and reached over to squeeze her hand gently. "I had my fingers crossed that you'd say 'yes'. I'll pick you up Saturday morning around ten. I'll be heading out about noon and should be back Sunday by dinner time."

"And that's the ten-cent tour. What do you think of the place?"

"Oh Alan, it's lovely. You're so fortunate to live in this cozy bungalow. And you have a lovely little garden out back, I can't wait to lounge there in the afternoon and read."

"I'm glad you like it. It was my parent's. I decided to keep the place after they passed away. It was difficult at first living here, but now I'm glad I stayed." He handed her the house keys, glancing at his wristwatch as he did so. "Whoa, look at the time, I should be on my way. The boys will be waiting for me."

They made their way to the front entrance. At the doorway, he turned to her and held her briefly, kissing her lightly on the forehead before letting her go. With a warm smile, she reached out and took his hand, saying, "Thank you, Alan, for all that you've done for me."

"No need to thank me," he replied in his pleasant voice. He swung the rucksack over his shoulder and then reached for his fishing pole and tackle box. "Enjoy the place. I'll see you Sunday evening." As he stepped out, he added, "Oh, I almost forgot, I left you some cold cuts and cheese in the fridge for your lunch this weekend."

"Thanks...and have a great time. I want to hear all about it when you get back, including the story about the big one that got away." She waved goodbye as the car backed out of the driveway.

What a wonderful man, she thought, shutting the front door behind her, *I really must do something to show my appreciation for all he's done for me.* She went to hang the keys on the hook next to the doorway and noticed one of the three keys was different, not at all like a house key.

An idea suddenly came to her. *This must be the key for the small storage room downstairs. Alan said the room's a mess and that he can't get himself to tidy it. I'm sure he'd appreciate it if I did the chore for him.*

The key unlocked the basement door. From what little she could see by the faint light filtering through the open door, the room appeared almost empty.

She fumbled for the light switch. It was a good deal further in from the door entrance than she expected. Once the lights flickered on, she gasped, then let out a piercing scream. Five white faces were hanging on the wall across from her, staring at her with blank eyes. She stumbled back as she caught her breath, looking on in horrified amazement at the faces.

Masks, she reassured herself, *they're just plaster masks.*

Cautiously, she made her way forward, her eyes fixated on the first mask, that of a young man. His eyes were shut, not staring as was her first impression. A small bronze plaque under the mask was inscribed with the word 'Apollo'.

She studied his facial features carefully. *He's beautiful, the face one would expect on a classical sculpture of the god Apollo.* Reaching out and gently running her fingers over his cheeks, she could feel the small bumps produced by a man's stubble. The sensation made her sick to her stomach.

"My God," she murmured in a trembling voice, "this was made from the face of an actual person. Why would Alan have these—" A sudden realization hit her. She staggered to one side, reaching out and grabbing onto a small bookshelf to stop herself from falling. *Death masks...the man is creating death masks from the corpses he embalms.* Clasping her hand tightly over her mouth, she suppressed the urge to be sick.

Her breathing had calmed a few minutes later. Some loose pages lay on the floor, having fallen from the bookshelf earlier. One was a reproduction of a painting of Neptune looking disapprovingly at another goddess. A goddess whose face not only looked remarkably like hers, but displayed her innocent, carefree expression as well. Picking up the paper, she looked over the writing along the bottom edge.

Dispute between Minerva and Neptune over the Naming of the City of Athens
Oil on canvas, 1689
René-Antoine Houasse

Making her way along the row of masks, she read the names on the plaques; *Apollo, Mercury, Artemis, Mars, Vesta.* The final plaque had no mask above it. It was inscribed with the name *Minerva.*

Mary sat at the kitchen table, staring out the back window. Even in her bewilderment she realized he planned to kill her. Death masks are made from the faces of the deceased. His charm had blinded her. The occasional look of admiration in his eyes was not for her, but for some perverse longing for an ancient goddess. The thought of Alan embalming her naked body only to steal the imprint of her face and lock it away in a dim room for his pleasure both sickened and angered her.

She dismissed the thought with a shudder and pondered what she should do. The fishing trip with friends had to be a lie. He would be back tonight to do away with her, only to return Sunday evening to 'discover' her murdered body. He'd probably make it look like a break-in. The police would conclude I awoke to find a burglar in my room, panicked, and got stabbed as I tried to flee. Of course they would find no injuries to my face, only a lone stab wound in my back.

The room suddenly felt stifling, so she made her way to the backyard. The daylight was waning and there was a slight chill in the air. For a moment she thought about her hunting trips with father, the warm afternoons followed by cool evenings. What was it he told her the first time they went hunting? 'You can be the hunter, or the hunted. I choose to hunt.'

"Yes..." Mary said slowly, trying to arrange her thoughts in order. "Father was right...be the hunter."

At three in the morning, Alan silently unlocked the side door and entered his house. Under his jacket, a large hunting knife was clipped to his belt.

A police vehicle was parked in Alan's driveway, two others were on the street.

"Jesus," swore the detective under his breath as he examined the dead body lying on the kitchen table. "What a bloody mess." After a moment's pause, he looked over at his sergeant and asked, "What was the cause of death? And what the hell happened to his face?"

"Struck by a heavy object from behind," answered the sergeant. "Crushed a good chunk of the skull. The hunting knife that did the rest of the damage to his face was his own. You can see the sheath clipped to his belt. And God only knows why the killer placed a cutting board under the head."

"Certainly not the most comfortable of pillows, but it's not likely he'll notice now," the detective pointed out sarcastically.

"Excuse me, Detective Conroy?" came a voice from the top of the basement steps.

The detective looked over his shoulder. "I'm detective Conroy," he replied.

The constable said; "We found something downstairs you should take a look at."

"What are those? Masks?" asked Detective Conroy as he entered the room, pointing to the far wall.

"The white ones are," confirmed the constable.

The detective took a pencil form his jacket pocket and walked up to what looked like a rag hanging at the end of the row of masks. He inserted the pencil into a hole near the edge of the rag and stretched it out.

The hollowed face of Alan Brown stared at the detective, the pencil was jutting into one of the eye cavities. "Skinned the poor bastard's face clean off," he murmured. "Took some skill to do this."

He didn't notice that below the small bronze plaque inscribed with the name of the goddess *Minerva* there was another name lightly scrawled in pen. That of *Ultio*, the goddess of revenge.

A TAROT PROPHECY

London, 1899

A single tear lands on the glass surface. Delicately, she brushes it away with her finger, then brings the photo to her lips and presses a soft kiss upon it.

"I miss you painfully, my love," she whispers, "but be patient a little while longer. I will have you home soon—I promise." With a trembling sigh, she gently sets the photo back onto the fireplace mantel, then turns and quietly walks out of the room.

Lady Bargrave gave a quarter turn to the key of the gas light. A faint yellow light illumined the area next to the round mahogany table. She and her guests had been sitting in the darkened room for the better part of an hour. Turning the gas on full would be an assault to the eyes.

The séance went extraordinarily well today, thought Lady Bargrave as she returned to her seat. *Elizabeth was in top form, calling forth four—or was it five?—spirits. She even managed to impress old Major Ellingwood, who normally ended each séance by exclaiming 'It's all a load of poppycock if you ask me!'. But not this time. The message from his old war comrade gave him quite a start. Something the spirit said, something only the Major understood. I wonder what it was...*

"Shall we conduct the next séance at my residence?" asked Lady Whitfield in her distinctively high, nasal tone.

"I have no objection," replied Elizabeth.

"Suits me just fine," added the Major.

Lady Padgett and Mrs. Garrett nodded their heads in the affirmative.

"Then it's settled," said Lady Bargrave with a smile. "We look forward to attending the next meeting at your charming residence."

"How splendid!" exclaimed Lady Whitfield with a squeak., clapping her hands together. "Then I shall expect each of you at my place in a fortnight." Turning to Elizabeth she added, "I do hope it's all right if my husband attends the séance as well? He can be a bit obstinate at times..." she paused ever so slightly and shot a sideways glance at the Major before continuing, "but he has agreed to attend with an open mind."

"Well then," Elizabeth answered in a reassuring voice, "it will be a pleasure to make the acquaintance of your husband and I'm sure he'll make an excellent addition to our group."

"Oh, thank you! He will be so pleased to hear it."

At this point, Lady Bargrave rose from her seat and parted the rich velvet curtains of the main window before saying;

"And now, let us head to the drawing room for our afternoon tea. I've requested a bottle of sherry and a nice claret to accompany our usual selection of sweets and savouries. I hope no one has any objections?"

"Not a single one, my dear lady!" the major exclaimed with a jovial voice. "Come ladies, let me have the honour of accompanying you to the drawing room."

The guests had departed by half-past six, all save for Elizabeth, who Lady Bargrave had discreetly asked during tea if she could stay behind.

"Dear me," said Lady Bargrave as she made her way from the reception hall, "It takes some effort to get Major Ellingwood out the door. There's no stopping him from recounting his war stories once he's had a glass or two of sherry."

"Or three," Elizabeth said with a sly grin.

The two women shared a laugh as Lady Bargrave slipped a hand through Elizabeth's arm and led her to the study.

Motioning to the chair in front of the desk, Lady Bargrave said; "Please have a seat here,

Elizabeth. I would value your opinion on a rather peculiar letter I received the other day."

Making her way around the desk, Lady Bargrave removed a cream-coloured envelope from the drawer, placing it facedown on the surface.

"Before I show you its contents, I would like to confirm my understanding that you have performed tarot readings in the past?"

"Why yes, I have...but how did you know?"

"You did a reading for a dear friend of mine, who spoke very highly of your abilities. Do you still read cards?"

"On occasion, yes."

"Then I'm curious to hear your thoughts on the contents of this envelope."

With a delicate touch, Lady Bargrave reached into the envelope and withdrew a few oversized playing cards, their backs facing upwards. Elizabeth took them from Lady Bargrave's outstretched hand and flipped them over, revealing three tarot cards. She read each out loud slowly, with emphasis, before placing them in a row onto the desk.

"The Magician...Death...The Lovers."

There was a heavy silence for several moments as the women focused on the sequence of cards before them. It was Elizabeth who spoke first;

"How curious...and you say the letter was addressed to you? Do you know who sent it?"

"Unfortunately, I do not. The penmanship is neat and the envelope itself is of very good paper, although the gilded edges are somewhat out of fashion by today's standards. The postmark is from Essex, but the district is smudged. I think it begins with the letter 'B'—or perhaps it's a 'P'—and ends with an 'E'.

Elizabeth shook her head. "I have no idea what the district could be. I've only been to Essex once or twice as a child."

"It does not matter. As it happens, I have promised to accompany Lady Whitfield to Essex later this week. We are to visit her ailing aunt. Perhaps she will suggest a district, not that it will help in identifying who sent the letter." Turning her attention back to the tarot cards, Lady Bargrave asked;

"What do you make of the cards? Why would anyone send them to me?"

"I believe someone has mailed you a three-card tarot spread. I can't fathom why, but I don't think there is any malintent behind it. Are the cards still in the same order as when you first opened the letter?"

"Why yes. I took one look at them and promptly replaced them back in the envelope. To tell you the truth, a strange feeling of superstitious dread crept over me the moment I touched the cards."

"There is no need for you to feel any apprehension, Lady Bargrave. As I said, I don't believe anyone has meant you harm by sending them." Looking down once more at the cards, she added in a softer voice, "Would you like me to proceed with a reading?"

Lady Bargrave remained silent for a moment, then replied uneasily, "If you would be so kind, Elizabeth."

Elizabeth shifted her chair slightly so that she was sitting directly in front of the cards. Leaning forward, she tapped her finger on the first of the three cards and slid it slightly towards her. "This card represents your past. The Magician stands for power and resourcefulness, traits which have served you well. You have managed your inheritance skillfully and have married a man of military distinction. All in all, you have few, if any, regrets concerning past decisions." She returned the card to its original position before sliding the next one forward. "The second card symbolizes the present and is represented by the Death—" She stopped herself as she heard Lady Bargrave catch her breath sharply.

"Don't be alarmed," Elizabeth said reassuringly, "The card is in an upright position, signifying a new beginning rather than the end. You have, or will soon encounter some change in your life, which may turn out to be a blessing in disguise." She glanced up at Lady Bargrave and noticed she had a distant look in her eyes, as if she were lost in thought. At length, Lady Bargrave said; "Please go on."

"The final card, The Lovers, signifies the future. There is a great potential for happiness through a new relationship. You must trust your heart."

"Charles told me to trust my heart once," Lady Bargrave said softly to herself after a moment's reflection.

"Forgive me, Lady Bargrave, but I didn't quite catch what you said."

"It's of no importance, I was speaking to myself." Getting up from her seat, she smiled and said, "Thank you so much for your time, Elizabeth. I feel so much better after your reading. I can sleep peacefully tonight knowing dark omens do not lurk in my future."

"None whatever, Lady Bargrave." Elizabeth stood up and the two women made their way to the front entrance. Before leaving, Elizabeth turned to her host and said;

"Lady Bargrave, I'll be attending a garden party next weekend hosted on behalf of an acquaintance of mine. Please don't think me presumptuous, but I believe you would enjoy attending the gathering with me. With your husband away in South Africa fighting in the Boer War, I can only imagine how lonely you must feel at times. I know my friend would be delighted to meet you. His name is Monsieur Cavellier, a most—"

"Antoine Cavellier?" interrupted Lady Bargrave.

"You know him?" Elizabeth asked, surprised.

"I know of him. He is a medium of exceptional ability. An aunt of mine attended one of his séances in France last year. She told me his powers go beyond that of just communicating with the departed, he can also..." She stopped herself, then said laughingly, "I'm so sorry Elizabeth. Look at me going on like some old gossiping maid. Thank you, I would be delighted to accompany you to the event. It really is most considerate of you to invite me. I'll arrange to send my carriage for you so that we may arrive together."

The party took place on a perfect afternoon, with bright blue skies and a gentle southerly breeze. The elegant marquee, adorned with blue, white, and red bunting, was already filled with guests by the time Elizabeth and Lady Bargrave arrived.

"I didn't realize Monsieur Cavellier was so popular, there must be close to fifty people present," observed Lady Bargrave.

"He is very well known in France and is rapidly gaining recognition as a leading spiritualist here in London as well. This gathering is being hosted by Sir William, a staunch supporter of the spiritualist movement. Some prominent physicians, professors, and lawyers are sure to be among the invited guests." A bright smile spread across Elizabeth's face as she added suddenly, "Ah, here comes our talented medium now."

Monsieur Cavellier was a handsome man, tall, strongly built, with thick, black wavy hair. As he approached, Lady Bargrave took note of his slender yet gentle face, highlighted by prominent cheekbones. A sense of calm seemed to emanate from his deep, pale gray eyes.

"Monsieur Cavellier, I would like to introduce Lady Bargrave."

"Enchanté," he said, taking her hand gently, bowing slightly as he did so.

"A pleasure to make your acquaintance Monsieur Cavellier, and thank you for having me."

"The pleasure is all mine, Lady Bargrave. Elizabeth speaks very highly of you and has told me all about the very successful séances you have hosted for her. Perhaps in the future I too can participate in one."

"That would be an honour, Monsieur Cavellier."

"Then I very much look forward to attending a session in the near future. But how rude of me to keep the both of you standing about. Allow me to bring you some refreshments before I introduce you to a few of my guests, some of whom I'm certain you'll find most fascinating."

Following the introductions, the guests were treated to a delectable meal consisting of Lobster Mayonnaise, Oyster Puffs, and delicately sweetened American Blancmanges for dessert. This was followed by additional refreshments and a performance by a string quartet. As the hour of six drew near, the guests started to depart at a leisurely pace.

"It's such a lovely afternoon, I don't want to leave just yet," said Elizabeth.

"I agree," replied Lady Bargrave. "It looks pleasantly shaded under that row of Hawthorn trees. Let's us walk there."

"Do you mind if I join you?" a familiar voice said from behind.

Both women turned and smiled at Monsieur Cavellier.

"Of course you may, if it's alright with you, Lady Bargrave."

"Your company would be most welcomed, Monsieur Cavellier," agreed Lady Bargrave.

"Thank you. But please, as my friends, you must address me by my Christian name, Antoine."

"Very well, Antoine it is," replied Elizabeth. "And now Antoine, if you wouldn't mind, could you go on ahead of us? Lady Bargrave and I have some gossip to catch up on."

Lady Bargrave let out a soft chuckle and tapped Elizabeth lightly on her forearm. "You really are naughty, Elizabeth. What will Antoine think of us?"

"I have already made up my mind that the two of you are wonderful, and no amount of gossiping on your part can change that. You will find me waiting for you just ahead of the first tree, basking in what remains of the afternoon sunshine."

After making their way to Antoine, the three of them spent the better part of an hour leisurely walking back and forth among the grassy path that meandered among the copse of trees. Their conversation was a pleasant one, each taking turns to tell the others a little more about their lives.

"You've lived a most fascinating life for one who has yet to turn thirty," observed Lady Bargrave.

"True," replied Antoine, "I have traveled and met some interesting people, but the life of a medium is not an easy one. Some sessions take a terrible toll on the body. Elizabeth can attest to that."

"I do not have your capabilities, Antoine. While some sessions leave me feeling drained for the remainder of the day, I'm aware that you have been bed ridden for a week or more following a materialization."

"I hope not to do many more of those, Elizabeth. The Society for Psychical Research is pressing me for a demonstration, but I think I will decline."

Both women encouraged him to remain steadfast on his decision.

"But let us not end such a beautiful day talking about such matters. Instead, I would like to invite the two of you to a picnic next weekend, if it agrees with your schedules."

"I have nothing planned," replied Elizabeth. "Lady Bargrave?"

Lady Bargrave hesitated slightly before answering. "Well...I'm not sure—"

"Oh please, do come," interjected Elizabeth, reaching out and taking Lady Bargrave's hand in hers. "We would miss your company terribly if you didn't join us."

"Yes, please say you'll accept my invitation," added Antoine softly.

"Very well," said Lady Bargrave after a moment, "I will join the two of you on a picnic next weekend."

"Très bien! Please leave all the arrangements with me. I know an excellent French chef in the city who would be delighted to prepare a picnic basket for such wonderful women as yourselves. I will send you both a proper invitation by mid-week."

"Thank you, Antoine," said Lady Bargrave, before raising a hand to her lips to suppress a yawn. "I'm so sorry, all this fresh air has made me a bit sleepy. I think I'll return to the marquee to bid my farewell to Sir William."

"I will join you, Lady Bargrave. Are you coming Antoine?"

"No, I think I'll stay and walk the grounds a bit longer. Sir William and I will be meeting a little later to discuss today's event. I guess it's the men's turn to gossip, n'est-ce pas?

Both women laughed, bid him farewell, then went on their way. Antoine stood and watched them for a short time. He thought; *Elizabeth is right, Lady Bargrave is quite a hand-some woman. Tall and slender with graceful movements. A radiant, lovely face as well. Yes, a beautiful woman, and quite wealthy too...*

The three met on several more occasions following that afternoon. It was clear that each enjoyed the others' company. It was also becoming evident to Lady Bargrave that Antoine was taking more than a passing interest in her. Elizabeth noted this as well, and on a few occasions politely excused herself from attending their planned outings, so that the two could spend time alone together.

In the weeks following Sir William's social event, Lady Bargrave hosted one of her own in order to introduce Antoine to several well-to-do individuals, many of whom were keenly interested in contacting their dearly departed. It was following the meal that Antoine noticed her absence. He made his way to the study, tapping gently on the door as he entered. Lady Bargrave was standing behind the desk, staring out of the large bay window, lost in thought. At the sound of the door opening, she looked over her shoulder and smiled at him.

"No need to knock, Antoine," she said softly.

He came up close to her and encircled his arms around her waist before kissing her lightly on the shoulder.

"I can tell something has been on your mind all day. Has it to do with us?" he asked in a concerned tone. "Perhaps you are having doubts as to the direction our relationship is heading?"

"None, Antoine. As the tarot reading foretold, I have 'followed my heart' and it has led me to you." With her gaze still fixed towards the window, she quietly murmured under her breath, "And may God forgive me..." She gently freed herself from his embrace and turned towards the desk, removing a letter from its drawer. Before handing it to him, she said, "In some ways, this simplifies matters between us..."

He could tell she was trying to hold back tears as he reluctantly accepted the letter from her. It read, in part;

...WISHES TO EXPRESS HIS DEEP REGRET THAT YOUR HUSBAND, LIEUTENANT GENERAL SIR CHARLES BARGRAVE, IS PRESUMED TO HAVE BEEN KILLED...I EXTEND TO YOU MY SINCERE SYMPATHY ON YOUR GREAT LOSS...YOUR HUSBAND DIED WHILE SERVING HIS COUNTRY...

After finishing the letter, Antoine lifted his head and spoke her name softly. She came to him and placed her head on his shoulder. He held her for a moment, then released her as she stepped back to look at him. With a solemn expression she said;

"I have a great favour to ask of you, Antoine, one I fear you will not like."

"Feel free to ask anything of me. You know I will do whatever I can to help you."

Lady Bargrave turned and began to pace the room, her fingers nervously tracing the delicate fabric of her handkerchief. Turning to face him once more, she hesitated slightly before asking;

"I...would like you to perform a materialization. I know you are one of the few who can call forth a complete person—not as a spiritual being, but as a *physical* one."

A heavy silence fell upon the room, lingering for what seemed an eternity before Antoine asked, somewhat hesitantly, "How...do you know this?"

"My aunt was present at the Bayeux séance last year. She witnessed your materialization of Professor Dubois' wife. Her exact words to me were, '*...as we stand here now, she was as alive as you and me. I spoke to her and held her hand. Her materialization lasted for a full ten minutes!*' I want you to bring back my husband. I want to hold his hand and look him in the eyes as I say my final farewell, and to reassure him that he need not worry about me as I am fortunate to have discovered friends who will look out for me."

She crossed the room to where Antoine was still standing. She reached up and caressed his cheek before kissing him tenderly. "Will you do this for me, Antoine? I feel it is the only way I can move forward in our relationship with a clear conscious."

He nodded his head slowly, then added;

"It will take a week or more for me to fully recover after such a demanding materialization. I'll expect you to tend to me like a mother hen during this time."

She smiled and once again caressed his cheek. "I will. And let us not delay—I propose that we hold our session this week. Best to have it at your residence so that I can tuck you into bed and care for you immediately afterwards. Oh...and please invite Elizabeth, it would be prudent to have another talented medium in the room with us." She took his hand in hers and led him to the door. "Come, it's time you rejoined our guests before they begin to wonder where you have disappeared to. I will follow you in a few minutes." Quietly closing the door behind him, she made her way to the desk and steadied herself on the back of a chair as the stark realization of what lay ahead over-took her.

The dimly lit parlor was illuminated by a few flickering candles, creating gentle shadows that danced across the green damask wallpaper that adorned its walls. In the far corner, across from the entrance, a lone candle sat atop a small mahogany coffee table. A few feet to the right of the candle, in a Hepplewhite armchair, sat Antoine. He had removed his jacket and vest, and his shirt sleeves were rolled up to his elbows. There were several large, white handkerchiefs on his lap. He beckoned for Elizabeth and Lady Bargrave to enter the room with a slight nod of his head.

"My dear ladies," he began solemnly as they approached him, "there remains but one task for you to do before I can begin." Handing the handkerchiefs to the two women, he continued, "With these, you must bind my wrists and ankles, *quite firmly*, to the chair. Any unexpected movement on my part could sever the ectoplasmic stream that will flow from my body to the materialization of General Bargrave. The consequences, I fear, would be most dire if this were to happen."

In silence, the two women did as they were told, after which Lady Bargrave kissed Antoine delicately on the cheek and whispered in his ear, "Thank you my dear. All will go well and soon we'll be together." She squeezed his hand before heading to the round table situated in the centre of the room. Elizabeth was already seated at one of the two chairs facing Antoine.

"You look incredibly pale, my dear," Lady Bargrave commented as she approached Elizabeth. "I brought a bottle of sherry here yesterday when I came to help Antoine set-up the room. Let's have a glass now. I think it will help to calm our nerves and restore your colour." Resting on the mantelpiece was the sherry bottle, accompanied by two crystal glasses. Lady Bargrave filled them close to the rim and offered one to Elizabeth. "Drink up and don't worry yourself so. I can feel it in my bones that everything will turn out right."

"Listen to Lady Bargrave, Elizabeth," added Antoine in a reassuring tone. "She is correct—nothing will go wrong. Just sit back and enjoy your glass of sherry." He gazed at his hands and then his feet, forcefully trying to free himself from the bindings. "You have done an excellent job securing me to the chair, ladies, so let us begin. I will commence by entering a state of meditation during which time I will summon my spirit guide, who will help me channel General Bargrave's spirit into a physical form. Do not communicate with me once I begin this process. The ectoplasm will exude from within me shortly thereafter, first from my mouth, then through my nose as well. The full materialization of General Bargrave from the ectoplasm will take at least a quarter of an hour. Once he is present, you may communicate with him, embrace him gently, but only for a short time." He was looking directly at Lady Bargrave as he said this. "I will not be able to sustain his presence here much beyond that time, as my own body will rapidly begin to weaken." With these final words he closed his eyes, calmed his breathing, and prepared to invoke his spirit guide.

Lady Bargrave turned her attention towards Elizabeth, who was rubbing her eyes with the back of her fingers. Placing a hand gently on Elizabeth's shoulder, Lady Bargrave asked;

"What's the matter Elizabeth? Are you not feeling well?"

"I feel...very lightheaded all of a sudden. Perhaps the sherry was...too much for me," she replied in a weak, unsteady voice.

"Yes, it was indeed too much. You see Elizabeth, I'm afraid I added a fair amount of morphine powder to your drink. But there's little you can do about it now, so just accept the fact that you will be sound asleep in a little while."

"What...what are you...saying," Elizabeth stammered, trying to keep her focus on Lady Bargrave.

"I guess I do owe you an explanation, even though your addled mind may understand little of what I'm about to recount." Shifting in her seat, Lady Bargrave turned to Elizabeth and continued in a steady, but subdued tone.

"The day of the tarot reading I told you that Lady Whitfield and I were leaving to visit her ailing aunt in Essex. She lives in the town of Braintree, where we stopped to purchase a few items for her before our arrival. I happened to enter a Stationer that, to my astonishment, sold cream-coloured envelopes...with gilded edges. 'How odd,' I thought to myself, 'these bare a striking resemblance to the envelope I received.' It was then that I recalled the Essex postmark on the letter, the smudged district beginning with the letter 'B' and ending in 'E'. Just like the name of the village I was in—*Braintree*. I went up to the sales clerk and told her a tale about wanting to buy the envelopes to send out as invitations, but was afraid friends of mine may have already purchased the same ones for their event. Had anyone purchased them recently, I inquired. She replied, 'Oh yes, a lovely couple was in here just over a week ago, I remember them quite well. The French gentleman was so charming, telling me I was très belle and that I should go to Paris to become a fashion model—imagine that! But they only purchased one envelope, so it couldn't be for invitations…'"

Lady Bargrave paused to glance over at Antoine. She watched in fascination as streams of fluorescent mist poured from his mouth and nose, gradually solidifying and gathering form just a few feet away from his chair. The materialization of her husband had begun.

Turning her attention back to Elizabeth, she continued;

"I went to a Private Inquiry Office upon my return to London the next day. I fabricated a tale that Antoine, who had proposed to my niece, was suspected of being unfaithful. The following afternoon they informed me that a woman, who matched your description in every detail, visited Antoine's home the previous evening, and did not leave until the next morning, when she was observed to have 'affectionately kissed the gentleman before her departure.'"

Lady Bargrave shook her head disapprovingly at Elizabeth. "You tried to deceive me, Elizabeth," she went on after a moment's pause. "You knew I was a strong believer in your powers, so you sent me those tarot cards, knowing I would accept your interpretation of what was to come. You introduced me to Antoine, who played his role as the seducer flawlessly. Soon I would be under his spell, funding his travels and expenditures as his reputation as the foremost medium flourished, all the while he would share this newfound wealth with you, his true love. The two of you would live a comfortable life at my expense. But the worst news was yet to come. The letter informing me of my husband's death arrived on the same afternoon I learned about your treacherous behaviour. My life came crashing down at that moment. My husband was dead, and I was being cruelly deceived by someone I trusted wholeheartedly.

"And then, for the second time that week, Providence played a role. A ray of sunlight was streaming through the bay window, illuminating the corner of my desk where the pile of tarot cards still sat. The Magician was the topmost card. The card that represents resourcefulness, that which I have practiced my entire life.

"It was then that I decided not to tell anyone of my husband's death, not until weeks later when I presented the letter to Antoine that ultimately convinced him to perform the materialization of my husband. Up until then, I went along with your scheme, pretending to be seduced by Antoine, waiting patiently for this day to arrive."

There was a flicker of terror in Elizabeth's eyes before her lids slowly closed and her head slumped forward.

"Enjoy your sleep Elizabeth, as it will be your last. Regrettably, I will need to set the room ablaze before I leave. The authorities will be none the wiser as to the cause of the fire. They will conclude that two mediums were in a trance when a candle toppled over and sparked a fire, engulfing them in smoke and flames while they remained oblivious to their surroundings. But first I plan to free my husband from Antoine, so that once again he can join me in this world as a *living person*, as my beloved husband. We shall begin a new life, perhaps in Australia, where no one will know us."

She looked over at the spot where the ectoplasm had been accumulating. Her husband was now standing there, the luminous nature of his body slowing fading, becoming more human, *more alive*, with each passing minute. He was in full uniform, his clothes and face stained with mud and gunpowder, just as if he had been whisked away from the battlefield at that instance.

"Oh Charles, it's really you my love," she whispered, holding back tears of joy. "I have one last task, sadly an unpleasant one, before I can free you. Then we will be together again."

She made her way to the fireplace and retrieved the kitchen knife she had secreted behind the mantel clock the day before. Taking a deep breath, she gathered her courage and with determined steps walked towards Antoine. Without hesitation, in one swift motion, she cut through the strands of ectoplasm that lay between him and her husband. Nothing could have prepared her for the violent response that followed.

Antoine's body convulsed as if shocked by a powerful electric current. Strands of ectoplasm soaked in blood spewed from his mouth. The chair started to splinter as the intensity of his convulsions increased. She heard the sickening sound of his shoulders dislocate form their sockets as his torso lurched forward, followed by the breaking of the bones in his wrists. One last violent heave arched his back to such an extent that she was sure it would snap in two. He remained in that monstrous position for a few horrible moments, then collapsed into his chair like a discarded marionette, his gray, blood-stained eyes staring vacantly at the ceiling.

Lady Bargrave remained frozen with fear, unable to avert her gaze from Antoine's broken body. An ashen hue took over her complexion as rapid, shallow breaths escaped her lips. Her legs were growing weaker and she swayed slightly, the knife slipping from her grasp. Its sudden clatter on the floor jolted her back to her present surroundings. She turned and ran to her husband, wrapping her arms around his neck, holding him close for a brief moment before backing away slowly, her hands clasped tightly over her mouth as if to choke back a scream, her head moving slowly from side to side.

"Forgive me Charles..." she cried under her breath, "Dear God, what have I done..."

General Bargrave displayed no emotion, his eyes appeared to look right through her. And as if in reply to her question, the General's jaw suddenly dropped revealing a gaping hole, allowing Lady Bargrave to see through to the green wallpaper behind him.

General Bargrave had indeed returned, returned from his resting place in the battlefield where he fell to enemy fire, a pointed shard of shrapnel having lopped off the back of his head. What stood in front of Lady Bargrave was his living corpse.

THE RECRUITER

Korean War, 1952

This was turning out to be one hell of a recon mission. We were an hour into our patrol when our squad was ambushed by a small group of enemy soldiers. The exchange of fire was over in a matter of minutes, leaving one of our guys wounded and another dead. This left us with a squadron of 13 men. Soldiers are a superstitious lot, and we took this to be a bad omen, a sign that we would all be going home in body bags before the mission was over. Sarge ordered us to 'knock-it off with the doomsday talk,' but you could sense a dark cloud had set-tled over the squad—we were all kind of spooked. The weather turned nasty the follow-ing day, the winds high and cutting and the temperature continued to drop as the day wore on. It was a slow, hard slog up the windswept hills, and we spent the night shivering in our sleeping bags.

Despite the lack of sleep, we found our-selves in high spirits the next morning. We had received orders to end our patrol and head to base camp K-52, located 10 miles north-east of our current position. Sarge estimated our time of arrival at eighteen hundred hours. He had no idea how wrong he was.

It was around noon when we came to a nar-row footpath that led up a steep, densely wooded hill. We were ten minutes into our climb when Harris, for reasons unknown, de-cided to take a quick head count. Only 12 men were present.

"Jesus!" the Sergeant cursed, a deep red hue spreading across his features. "How the hell did no one notice a man missing? Goddammit, you're all sleepwalking—you really are going to send us home in body bags. Now wake up and tell me who the hell is missing!"

Without hesitation I said, "Connely, sir." I don't know how I knew, I just felt certain it was him.

"That's just great," Sarge barked. "Hand me your binoculars Taylor."

I removed them from around my neck and handed them to the Sarge. The men moved out of the way as he scanned back over the trail. It didn't take him long to spot Connely. "I've found the son-of-bitch. He's sitting by that burned out bunker we passed on the way here. Can't tell if he's passed out. He's probably numb with cold at this point."

Sarge handed back my binoculars, adding;

"Go and get him Taylor. Get some food in him and then get him back here on the double. There's a bit of a clearing just up ahead. We'll wait for you there. The men can eat their grub in the meantime."

I started back down the path. The wind picked up something fierce as I approached the bottom. A dust devil formed directly in front of me, sending leaves and debris flying through the air. I turned my back to it, and as I did, I was shocked at what I saw. Heavy thunder clouds hung over the hill, and a solid wall of snow, like a white veil of death, moved silently yet at a tremendous speed down the hill, engulfing the men and their surroundings in a matter of seconds.

I turned and ran for my life, heading straight for what remained of the bunker. There were still three or four pieces of roof timber in place, weighed down by a few sandbags. Connely was sitting motionless on the far edge of the bunker, his legs dangling into the interior. I simply tackled him, knocking both of us into the pit. We dropped a good five feet before hitting the hard, frozen earth with our backs. Connelly was out cold. As I got to my feet, I grabbed him by the collar and pulled him under the roof timbers with me. A moment later a powerful blast of cold hit us.

The next thing I recall is waking up in the morning, a rat the size of a cat having made its way onto my face. I scrambled to my feet in a hurry, cursing as the back of my head hit one of the ceiling logs. My entire body ached something fierce. I looked over at Connely who was still lying on his back, his face a pale blue hue. The poor bastard was dead. I knelt beside him and removed the ammo clip from his rifle, stashing it into my backpack. Given how bad things had turned out so far, I reasoned I would probably need it on my way to K-52.

I left Connely as he was and made my way out of the bunker. I was surprised at how little snow there was on the ground—just wisps of it drifting about. I would have expected a foot or two of the white stuff given the intensity of the storm. *Or was it a storm?* I thought uneasily. I shook the doubt from my mind as I made my way back to the footpath.

A heavy air of desolation hung over the area. "Now that's odd," I said under my breath. "No damage to the trees. Everything the same as when I left it yesterday. No sign that the men were ever here, not even a discarded ration tin..." I let the binoculars drop to my chest, reached into my pocket for one of the few cigarettes I had remaining and lit it. After a few deep puffs I told myself to get moving if I wanted to make camp before nightfall. I flicked my cigarette away, then slid the rifle from my shoulder and rested my finger on the trigger before starting up the path.

I stumbled upon a second path a few hours later, partly obstructed by some low-lying shrubs. I pushed aside the stems with the barrel of my rifle. There were several faint impressions visible on the patches of snow. I bent down for a closer look.

Combat boots, I murmured. *Looks like some of our troops came this way. Odds are good that this is the way to K-52. Certainly heading in an easterly direction. If the trail changes direction at any point, I'll just double back.*

It's Ironic how simple decisions can sometimes change your entire life. Stay on the current path or veer off to the right and follow the new path? It was my misfortune to choose the latter.

The new path held its easterly direction, but the further along I went, the more difficult it became to follow, as it meandered through heavily wooded areas. I had just pushed my way through some dense underbrush when I stepped into a clearing...and froze in my tracks. I swallowed hard against the tightening in my throat, my heart pounding in my chest. Thirty feet ahead of me sat a Korean soldier on a low wooden crate, his back towards me. He was sitting behind a mounted 50-caliber machine gun pointed in the direction of the valley below. A wall of stacked sandbags, about three feet high and in the shape of a half-moon, extended a few feet on either side of the gun.

My gut reaction was to step back through the bushes and retrace my footsteps to the original path. But I didn't. Instead, I stood there, a feeling of anger swelling up inside me. I was mad at myself for not staying on the original path, but what truly infuriated me was the sight of the soldier in front of me. *He* was the cause of all my troubles. I was lost in some god forsaken land, hungry, tired and aching all over. And *he* was blocking my way to base camp.

I raised my riffle and took aim at his head before walking slowly towards him. I didn't know a word in Korean, so when I got within ten feet of him, I shouted;

"Hand's up or I'll shoot!" To my surprise, he slowly lifted his hands in the air, stood up, and turned to face me. He wasn't fazed in the least, as if he had been expecting me.

I motioned with my rifle for him to move away from the machine gun. He took a few steps to the left then stopped. It was at that moment that I noticed the smirk on his face.

What's up with this guy? Does he think I'm joking? That I don't have the guts to put a bullet in him?

"What's so funny, asshole?" I snapped. "Don't think I have it in me to shoot you?" A killing rage was beginning to infect my heart.

He just stood there. The same stupid smirk on his lips. So I squeezed the trigger.

The bullet got him clean between the eyes, the back of his skull exploding outwards before he collapsed backwards.

I lowered my riffle and just stood there staring at the body. A saying came into my mind, one my grandmother, a very pious woman, used to recite to my mother on occasion, 'In the midst of life we are in death'. I guess there was some truth to what she said. I'm sure he wasn't expecting to die today.

My anger was beginning to subside. I lit my last cigarette and looked around as I let the smoke warm my lungs. It was then that I started to wonder what the hell a solitary soldier was doing here. What was he defending? Some bushes?

I went over and took a look at the machine gun. It looked new. It certainly had not been fired recently. I turned and made my way to the body. I found a folded sheet of paper in his jacket pocket. A coin was nestled within which dropped in the palm of my hand. It was about the size of a quarter and engraved with characters I didn't recognize. But I did recognize what it was made of. Bright, beautiful, gold.

"This has got be worth a pretty penny," I said to myself, as I ran the coin through my fingers. "So, this is what you were defending. There must be a stash of gold hidden somewhere nearby. Stolen loot that your government will help itself to at some point—happens in every war. What a dirty business."

I pocketed the coin then unfolded the sheet of paper to reveal a drawing of a crude map. The machine gun was clearly marked on the chart. *That simplifies things,* I murmured with a slight chuckle. Once I had the map correctly oriented, all I had to do was focus my binoculars on the area that aligned with the 'X' on the chart. And there it was, an entrance to a cave partially hidden by a cluster of trees.

Just a couple of hundred feet up, I told myself. *A bit steep near the entrance but I should have no trouble reaching it.*

It was an hour later when I finally made my way into the cave. I remained crouched just inside the entrance for several minutes, giving my eyes time to adapt to the low light. The cave itself was small and obviously man-made. It measured about 25 feet in diameter, while its height reached 10 feet. It had a few slits in the roof through which faint sunlight seeped in. The only object present was a wooden crate on the far wall opposite the entrance. I took one more careful look about, then started cautiously towards the crate, my rifle at the ready.

I stared down at it for a little while, considering the possibility that it might be booby trapped. "You didn't come this far just to walk away now," I told myself, "Get on with it."

With some apprehension, I used the barrel of my rifle to lift the lid. Nothing happened. I peered inside and let out a long, low whistle. Gold—and lots of it.

"You've struck it rich, you lucky son-of-a-gun," I congratulated myself out loud. "There must be a least a quarter million dollars' worth of gold here."

"Actually, more like half-a-million. There are several gold ingots beneath the coins."

I spun around in a sudden burst of fear, my gun trained on the spot where the voice originated. I was pointing my rifle at an old man, sitting on a narrow ledge carved into the rock face.

"No need to shoot. As you can see, I'm old and unarmed."

I stole a glance to either side of me as I kept the rifle aimed squarely at his head.

"Don't worry," the old man said reassuringly, "no one else is here."

I took a few wary steps towards him. "Who the hell are you? How did you get here?" I demanded.

"I've been here for several days. Sure beats wandering along some god forsaken trail that leads nowhere. Haven't moved from this spot since you arrived. I was surprised you didn't see me, guess your eyes weren't adjusted to the low light. Thought it best to keep quiet until now as I couldn't take the chance you'd shoot me thinking I was the enemy. As to who am I, I'm a recruiter. A damn good one I may add. I'm proud to say I'm a recruiter for *the best* army in the world."

"Like hell you are!"

"Oh, but I assure you Taylor, I am," he replied matter-of-factly.

My eyes narrowed, and I asked in a dangerously calm voice; "How do you know my name?"

"I know," the old man said earnestly, "because you said it out loud."

"Bullshit."

"Oh, but you did. You were looking down at the gold and said, 'You've struck it rich, Taylor, you lucky son-of-a-gun.'"

My mind raced as I tried to think back to that moment. *Did I mention my name? It certainly sounded like what I said.*

"Maybe I did say that..." I replied cautiously. I took another step forward before asking:

"What do you mean you're a recruiter for the best army. What army are you talking about?"

"Not only is it the best, but the largest army in the world as well, 'the number of whom is as of the sand of the sea.' Revelations 20:8, in case you're not familiar with the Good Book. I recruit special men for this elite force, men like yourself, who aren't afraid to kill, just like you weren't afraid to kill the unarmed guard at the base of the hill..."

"How do you know that?" I demanded, tightening my hold on the rifle as I advanced another step, bringing the muzzle to within a foot of the old man's head.

"You wouldn't be here if you didn't, now would you?"

A menacing grin crept onto his face, and his pupils seemed to darken into two bottomless voids. "Welcome to my army, Taylor. I'm sure the killing will be to your liking."

An ungodly laugh escapes from his sinister mouth, as the heat in the cave suddenly becomes unbearable. Beads of sweat run down my face and neck. The rifle turns red-hot, searing my skin, forcing me to release my grip. And as I do so, a yawning chasm opens beneath me. I cast one helpless look at the old man before the earth swallows me whole. As I descend, I let out a scream filled with madness in recollection of the last scene my eyes beheld. The old man had cloven hooves for feet.

Outside, a Korean soldier lying dead next to a machine gun opens his eyes. He gets up, brushes the snow off his pants and jacket, and seats himself on a small crate directly behind a machine gun. He checks his pockets to make sure his map and gold coin are once again in their proper place. Snow laden clouds begin to fill the sky. He lights a cigarette, inhales deeply, and stares straight ahead, waiting patiently for the next recruit to arrive.

SPIRIT PHOTOGRAPHY

Boston, 1862

"May I?" asked Mr. Burke, gesturing towards the étagère where a selection of photographs in mahogany frames was elegantly displayed.

Caroline Harmon nodded her head in approval, adding, "By all means."

Mr. Burke examined the photographs with keen interest. "Quite remarkable," he commented. "The lady next to you in this photograph, with her hand resting on your shoulder, you say is your great aunt?"

"Yes. She sailed on the Emerald from Waterford with fifty other passengers. The ship had a good reputation as a seaworthy vessel, and was ably navigated by Captain Maitland and his crew, who had made the voyage many times before. The ship left port on May tenth of the year 1835, and three weeks later it encountered rough seas as she approached the coast of Nova Scotia. All on board were lost. None of my aunt's possessions washed ashore in the weeks that followed, so that photograph of her departed spirit looking lovingly over my shoulder is all I have to remind me of her. It is such a comfort."

"I can well image, Mrs. Harmon. And you say the photographer with this remarkable ability to capture departed spirits is called John Hamilton?"

"Yes, that's correct. I know you are probably skeptical about the authenticity of the photographs, but I can assure you they are indeed real. The entire photographic procedure is above board. You can select from any of the glass plates in his studio and stay to observe him develop the photograph if you wish."

"I believe you, Mrs. Harmon. I do not question Mr. Hamilton's special abilities. If you would be so kind as to furnish me with his address, I would like to pay him a visit. I came across a collection of letters penned by my great aunt, who lived in Australia, to my mother. It was obvious to me that she admired my mother very much. She passed away soon after my own mother died of pneumonia when I was a child of ten. I know little of the woman, so to see her image captured in a photograph would mean a great deal to me."

"His studio is on Washington Street. I believe I slotted his business card onto the back of the picture frame you were just holding. Please help yourself to it, as I have another in my desk drawer."

"A pleasure to meet you, Mr. Burke. Please have a seat. Can I offer you a drink?" John Hamilton held the door to his studio open and waved his arm towards a pair of Windsor arm-chairs.

"Thank you, Mr. Hamilton. I'll partake in whatever you're having."

"Very well. I hope gin is to your liking."

Mr. Burke nodded his head as he seated himself. He glanced around the small studio before focusing his attention onto Mr. Hamilton as he poured the drinks. A man of medium build with a square face, friendly brown eyes and black wavy hair with the first signs of gray appearing at the temples. *The type of person no one would take notice of,* he thought.

"Here you are, Mr. Burke," John handed him the drink as he took the seat next to him. "You indicated in your correspondence that you had a great aunt who lived in Australia, and this is the dear soul you wish me to photograph to-day."

"That's correct. I know very little about her, except that she was very fond of my mother and inquired about me often in her correspondence with her. She referred to me as 'that precious little bear' as mother told her how

I foraged for berries whenever we strolled in the woods together. It would mean a great deal to me to have an image of this kind-hearted woman."

"Let us hope her departed soul graces us with an appearance," responded John, raising his glass towards Mr. Burke before taking a drink. "Note that I used the word 'hope' since I have no influence over the spirits themselves, so I cannot guarantee that we will photograph your great aunt. Unfortunately, there is no sign of a spiritual presence as I take the photograph, so it is only after the plate is developed that we'll know if her spirit was present."

"I understand. Mrs. Harmon had mentioned that such may be the case."

"Let us hope that it is not," John reassured him. "Once you have finished your drink, please have a seat in the plush armchair positioned in front of the silk panel. Take your time, as I will require several minutes to set-up the camera."

Once comfortably seated in the armchair, Mr. Burke was asked to remain as still as possible while Mr. Hamilton opened the shutter of the camera for a full minute. After the photograph was taken, the plate was developed in the dark room, the entire procedure not taking more than ten minutes.

"Congratulations, Mr. Burke," said John in an excited voice as he exited the dark room with the photograph in hand. "One of the more exceptional images I have managed to capture so far. Her spirit image is remarkably clear."

The image displayed a ghostly figure with well defined features standing next to the seated Mr. Burke. "This is truly remarkable," said Mr. Burke in awe as he accepted the photograph from John. He studied the image of his great aunt for several moments in silence. "A handsome woman, but there is a certain sadness in her eyes." He took his gaze away from the photograph and reached out to shake John's hand. "Thank you, Mr. Hamilton. You are blessed with an exceptional gift."

John couldn't help but feel smug as he treated himself to a French meal of ham in champagne sauce at the Parker House Hotel. It had been a good day. Mr. Burke was sure to mention his name to friends and colleagues, which would surely lead to more customers.

Having emptied his glass of the fine Hermitage wine, he leaned back in his chair and reflected on the afternoon's events;

That photo was quite remarkable. I've never had a spiritual image appear with such clarity. A beautiful woman, but as noted by Mr. Burke, a look of sadness in her eyes.

John lit his cigar and took several puffs as his thoughts returned to the photograph. *Why the sadness?* he pondered. *He did say she drowned at sea. Does a soul communicate its emotions through its eyes, which I am able to capture by way of my camera? But wasn't a soul to be at peace after death?*

His thoughts were interrupted by the presence of a waiter next to him.

"Excuse me, sir,"

"Yes?"

"A gentleman requests your company. He is seated next to the window closest to the entrance."

John tapped the ash from his cigar as he surveyed the area indicated by the waiter.

"Well I'll be," he said with an amused smile. "Tell the gentleman that I'll join him shortly."

"Very good, sir."

"I thought it was you, John," the handsome, middle-aged man said with a smile.

"What are you doing here, Robert? I thought you were in New York for the remainder of the week."

"That was the plan, but the judge decided to throw out the case against my client, so I find myself back in town early. But is this place not outside of your usual routine for a Monday evening?"

"It is," replied John with a sly smile as he took a seat next to his friend, "but I had a particularly good day at work and so decided to reward myself with a decadent meal."

"I am glad to hear it. Let us share a bottle of Port and you can tell me all about it."

John recounted his session of that afternoon, Robert listening with keen interest, knowing his wife, a staunch spiritualist, would want to know the smallest of details when he recounted the events to her.

"But enough about me, Robert, tell me about your stay in New York. Anything of interest happening in the city?"

"Not much since you were there last. Bustling as usual. Did you know its population has reached one million? We're not even two-hundred thousand in our city. Let me tell you, there's plenty of business to be had for lawyers in New York. I would not be surprised if our firm opens an office there soon. As to what is new and noteworthy, I'll let you read about that for yourself. I picked up a newspaper to read during the train ride. I'll leave it with you before we go."

The two men continued to converse until Robert noticed the restaurant had emptied.

"Good Lord, what time is it?" he asked, taking his watch from his vest pocket. A small, clover-shaped pendant fell to the ground as he did so. "A gift for my wife," he commented as he reached down to retrieve the pendant, "who, I fear, will be most upset at my late arrival home tonight."

Robert took a hansom cab to his residence, while John, who felt the need to clear his head from the effects of too much wine, favoured walking home, the newspaper tucked safely under his arm.

The following afternoon John was surprised to find Robert entering his studio.

"I'm sure you were not expecting to see me here so soon," commented Robert, smiling.

"I must admit I was not. Is everything alright?"

"Of course. I didn't mean to alarm you. I've actually come on business. The Post will be reporting on the McCarthy murder case. As I am one of the prosecuting lawyers, they asked for a photograph to use as a reference for their newspaper illustration."

"I appreciate the business, Robert. I'm available to take your photo now if that is convenient for you."

"Splendid. I have a bit of time before my next client meeting. I can come by tomorrow to collect the photograph."

A short time later, John stepped out of the dark room with a puzzled expression on his face. In addition to Robert, three other people appeared in the photograph. All three were women, depicted with exceptional clarity, just like the spirit in Mr. Burke's photograph.

How am I going to explain this? thought John, irritably. *The appearance of a single spirit is an uncommon enough event, and now I have three when I least desire them. A confounded nuisance. Best if I tell Robert the negative was underdeveloped and that I'll need to take another photograph.*

There was something about the women that disturbed John. Was there a look of fear in their eyes? And the woman to the left of Robert, why did she look familiar? Her face was heart-shaped, boasting high cheekbones, full lips, and deep eyes, her thick hair elegantly arranged under a large hat. *Best if I transfer the image to paper so that I can take a better look,* he decided.

Once the transfer was complete, John took a magnifying lens from his work bench and bent over the photograph. After a few minutes, he slowly straightened himself and placed the lens aside with an unsteady hand. "This cannot be," he murmured, as he made his way slowly to the armchairs at the front of the studio. He took up Robert's newspaper from the side table where he had left it earlier that morning. And there she was, the face of the woman that stood to the left of Robert in the photograph. The caption read, *Serial Killer Fear Grips City. Third Murder Victim Identified.*

He shut his eyes and ran his fingers across his forehead before reading further. On page two of the article, he saw what he had antic-ipated—the sketch of the two remaining vic-tims, both of whom appeared in Robert's photograph. He let the paper drop to the floor as he fell back into the chair.

"What am I to do?" he asked himself. "This is too horrible. These poor souls have made themselves know to me. But what can I do?" And then the thought occurred to him that *they chose to appear* in Robert's photograph.

"That must be it," he said thoughtfully, "They are asking for Robert to pursue justice on their behalf. He is well connected with the legal and law enforcement community in New York. It only makes sense he could help bring this fiend to justice."

John reached down and took the newspaper from the floor. He stared at the faces of the women for a long minute before stating; "I will do everything I can to help you." He then pondered silently; *The largest obstacle may be Robert himself. Unlike his wife, he remains a skeptic when it comes to spiritualism, and although we have known each other for many years, it would not surprise me if he questioned the authenticity of this photograph.* John folded the newspaper and tossed it onto the side table as he stood up and added hope-fully; "But I must convince him otherwise."

Robert came to collect his photograph the following day.

"Please have a seat, Robert. I need your opinion on a somewhat unique situation."

"Certainly, I'll be only to happy to help if I can."

John took a seat next to Robert and cleared his throat before beginning in a calm, even voice;

"I know you are a skeptic when it comes to spiritualism, Robert, and though you have never told me directly, I suspect you are suspi-cious of my own unique ability as well."

"Nonsense," replied Robert. "I may be a skeptic when it comes to spiritualism, but it in no way changes my high regard for you."

John nodded his head slowly in apprecia-tion before passing the photograph over to Robert, saying; "Have a look at this."

Robert took the photograph and suppressed an involuntary gasp when he saw the image.

After a pause, he asked; "What is the meaning of this, John?"

"Tell me Robert, do you recognize the women in this photograph?"

Returning the photo to John, he responded with a hint of anxiety, stating; "They appear familiar, but I am certain I have never met any of them before."

"Their images appeared in the newspaper you left with me the other day. They are all victims of a serial killer."

"Of course," he said with some relief. "I read the paper on the train. That's why their faces appear familiar. But why would they appear in my photograph?"

"Because I believe the woman in this photograph are asking for your help in apprehending the killer. You have prosecuted killers in the past, and your ties to the city's law enforcement community are strong."

"I'm sorry, John, but there is little I can do. The killer has not yet been apprehended, and unless he is from this city, I cannot prosecute anyone from New York."

John sat back and ran his hand through his hair as he thought the situation over. "You are correct, of course," he said eventually. "I suppose the best action now is to hand the photograph over to the police. Perhaps in some small way it may help with their investigation."

"I would advise against such a course of action," Robert cautioned him.

"What do you mean?" John asked with a puzzled expression.

"Look at it through the eyes of the police," began Robert. "They would be highly suspect of your spirit photography, believing it to be a form of photographic trickery, and will begin to question your motives for producing such a photograph. I'm afraid they may even consider you the murderer—"

"But that's preposterous!" John interrupted in disbelief.

"Is it? You have been to New York on several occasions these past several weeks, have you not?"

"Why yes, you know perfectly well that I have done several photography sessions in that city. Your own wife introduced me to a few customers."

"And so you had your photographic equipment with you."

"I did," replied John, a touch of uneasiness creeping into his voice.

"And you probably stayed on your own when you were there?"

"At hotels..."

"So your whereabouts in the evenings will be difficult for you to verify."

"Robert, you do not think for a moment that I—"

"I do not, but the police will see your actions as suspect. You could have photographed the women during your visits to New York, perhaps months previous to doing away with them. They will think it far too coincidental that you possess the images *of each of the victims.*"

"My God, Robert," John said uneasily after a moment's pause, "you have truly alarmed me. What do you recommend I do?"

Robert reached over and placed his hand reassuringly on John's shoulder. "I will think things over tonight. My suggestion at this point is to do nothing, but if you insist on going to the authorities, then you will follow my directions to the letter. Best if you leave the photograph with me for the time being."

"Thank you, Robert. You are a true friend."

John Hamilton stared vacantly at the empty brick wall in front of him. He sat alone in a jail cell, convicted in the killing of three women, to be executed by hanging in a week's time. He runs the events of that fateful day over and over in his mind, the absolute shock of seeing Robert enter his studio followed by four policemen. Robert did not say a word as John was arrested for suspicion of murder and escorted away in handcuffs. Not a single word.

During the trial, Robert's testimony was damming. He single handily built the prosecution's case from the witness box. Robert, who had been his dear friend for years, had sent him to the gallows.

What John will never know is that Robert stayed behind in the studio after he was escorted out by the police. Once alone, he lit a kerosene lamp and entered the dark room. Finding the original photographic plate, he placed it next to the lamp before removing a small, clover-shaped pendant from his pocket. He held it next to the image of the woman closest to the edge of the photograph. She was wearing the identical pendant.

"You have robbed me of my enjoyment, John," Robert said to himself, "I will need to behave myself in New York for quite some time. But I must admit, it would have been my neck in the noose in place of yours had you been more observant. Perhaps if you were a little more sober that evening, you would have recalled this pendant which I had dropped during our dinner." He ran the pendant several times through his fingers before returning it to his pocket, adding, "But what I found most surprising was that you, a portrait photographer, did not recognize the look in each of the women's eyes for its true nature—intense, unadulterated hate. Hatred for me."

He moved the lamp to one side before shattering the glass plate with a blow from his elbow. Collecting the pieces in his handkerchief, he left the studio and causally strolled towards Boston Harbor.

SECOND SKIN

Edinburgh, 1852

"Now this is odd," mused James Henderson as he reached for the small leather-bound volume sitting atop a row of books on the uppermost shelf of the Rare Book Room. It had no title and its leather binding was of a pale white hue, in contrast to the rich browns that bound the other books on the shelf. Securing the book under his arm, he descended the bookcase ladder and made his way to a small reading table positioned beneath one of the large windows on the opposite wall.

Now where did this book come from? he pondered, setting it on the table before taking a seat. *I've been acquiring rare books for the university library these past fifteen years, yet I can't recall coming across this volume on any of our shelves. Evidently someone felt it was important enough to include it in our collection. Mind you, if it is worth keeping, I don't see how I'm going to include it in our catalogue when it lacks both title and author.*

An hour went by as he perused the volume with keen interest.

This is indeed a very singular book, he concluded. *I would estimate its date as late sixteenth century, written in cipher, most likely a medical text. The illustrations are finely drawn, although some are of a grotesque nature. I must have William examine it. If anyone can decipher the text, it is he. I'll arrange to have dinner with him tonight at his club.*

James stifled a yawn as he closed the book. He felt lightheaded, prompting him to lean forward and rest his head on his hands. He had the sensation of a drop forming on the tip of his nose, and with a start realized that his nose was bleeding. Fumbling for his handkerchief in his trouser pocket, he cursed under his breath as he spotted the blood stains on the book's cover.

He pinched his nose through the fabric of the handkerchief and tilted his head back for a minute. *That should do it,* he reassured himself, *now to tend to the book.*

But there was not a hint of blood on the book, and what James found more curious was that the leather binding was no longer a pale white hue but had taken on a slight reddish tone. Or was it simply a trick of the light?

William Robertson was a practicing physician and lecturer to graduate students at the Royal Edinburgh Hospital. Fifteen years ago, Jame's grandmother had been admitted to the hospital, in actual fact an asylum for mentally ill patients, and it was there that James met William. The doctor was an avid collector of old medical texts and manuscripts, and when he learned that James was the curator of the university's Rare Book Room, it was inevitable that the two would form a strong friendship.

"Once again, I must thank you for agreeing to see me on such short notice, William."

"Think nothing of it, my dear friend. It has been far too long since we last dined together. I hope the venison was to your liking?"

"Quite so," replied James, after sipping the last of his port. "A most delicious meal."

"I'm glad you enjoyed it. And now, shall we make our way to the smoking room? You stated in your note that you have a rare book encoded in cipher that you wish me to examine. I must admit, you have certainly sparked my curiosity."

Once the two men were seated comfortably next to the fire and lit their pipes, James removed the linen handkerchief he had carefully wrapped around the book and handed the volume over to William.

"Before you look through it, I'm curious as to your opinion on the binding."

William ran his hand over the front and back cover before taking out his monocle to better inspect its quality.

"Hmm....there are several curious features, the most apparent being the absence of the title, or other text, anywhere on the exterior. I can't say from which animal the leather originated from, but is has, how shall I put it, an unusual yielding quality to it. Very odd for such an old book—late sixteenth century I believe you said?"

"Yes, that is my best estimate currently."

"As to the colour of the leather, I'm not really sure what to say. An off-white, with perhaps the slightest hint of crimson, although that may be due to the glow cast by the flames in the fireplace."

"Perhaps that is so," agreed James.

William proceeded to leaf through the volume, occasionally stopping to examine an illustration more closely with his monocle.

"Well?" asked James anxiously after several minutes had past.

"The images are quite interesting, depicting human dissections that would be unusual for that time period. As to the cipher employed, I can presently say little. I did spot two names near the end of the book—*Adrien* and *Michel*—both represented by the French spelling, so there's a good chance the original text is also in French. There are no abstract symbols to decipher, and most of the letters are from the Roman alphabet, both of which work to our advantage. Why don't I send you a note within a fortnight to inform you on my progress."

"Please do. Once you provide me with the substitution key—"

"*If* I'm able to provide you with one," interjected James. "Unfortunately, the rate of success is very low when it comes to deciphering such obscure texts."

"I have the utmost confidence you can do so, William. And when you do, I plan to devote my evening hours to translating the text. With any luck I should have the entire volume translated in a few months time."

"I'm flattered you value my ability so highly, James. Let us hope I do not disappoint you. I'll admit, I'm very curious as to its contents, and

I hope you will afford me the opportunity to read it once you have completed your task."

"Without question," nodded James.

"Excellent. Now, tell me about any new medical manuscripts you have acquired for the university. I happen to know that Sir Patrick has donated several from his private collection. Anything that may be of interest to me?"

Thirteen weeks later, William had successfully deciphered the codex. He was surprised at how quickly he accomplished the task.

"It's curious," he said to himself, as he leafed through the pages of the book. "I can't shake the vague feeling that I was being guided in some strange manner during this entire process. True, the cipher's one-for-one substitution rule made the decoding a relatively straight forward affair, yet I managed to make some extraordinary guesses along the way, far more than chance alone would dictate. Very queer. I'm beginning to wish that James never introduced me to this book. I shall feel more at ease once I get it back in his hands."

William was greeted with great enthusiasm when he visited James at his home the following day.

"Come in William. Let me take your hat and overcoat. What an exciting day this is! To break the cipher in three months time, a work of shear brilliance! There is an excellent bottle of Brandy awaiting us in my study. Follow me and let's toast to your success before we sit down and discuss how you decoded the cipher. I want to hear every detail."

But William was not keen to elaborate on the details. He wanted to be done with the book, so he recounted in very general terms the procedure he employed.

"So you see, James, a good deal of my success was due to sheer luck—far more than I was entitled to."

"Nonsense, you are far too modest. But I can see you are tired and not up to the task of explaining the details to me. I fully understand."

"Thank you. I think I'll be on my way, perhaps I can get some rest prior to giving my evening lecture to my students."

"Let me fetch your hat and overcoat and see you out. Please pay me another visit when you are up to it."

At the doorway, William hesitated. He turned to James and said in a serious tone;

"James, from the fragments of text I used to decipher the code, I got the distinct impression that it is not a medical book, but one that concerns itself with dark magic. I sense it is an evil book and no good can come from translating it. I would advise you to leave it alone."

"Nonsense! The Rare Book Library has several such books. You know as well as I do that it is all superstitious rot, but they are of historical importance nevertheless."

"Perhaps, but I believe you would do well by heeding my advice."

Before leaving, he paused once more to address William.

"I almost forgot," he went on, "there is a series of illustrations that depict the surgical removal of a swath of skin from the back of a cadaver. A small "V" shaped cut is visible on one of the edges of the removed skin. When I carefully examined the book's leather binding, I found the same "V" shaped cut in the lower inside corner of the back cover. I believe the book is bound in human skin."

"Anthropodermic bibliopegy," said James thoughtfully. "A gruesome practice but such books have crossed my path during my work at the university. Thank you for identifying it as such."

William gave a slight nod, then uttered, "Take care, my friend," as he departed.

As intended, James spent his evenings patiently deciphering the text. It was a slow and tedious process at first, but he soon found himself translating several pages during the course of a single evening. After a month of working well into the early hours of morning, he reached the section of the book William had made mention of, that which depicted the surgical removal of skin from a cadaver. William had been correct in his surmise, the book did deal with subjects of an uncanny nature. James was in disbelief at what the passage revealed. Could it be? There was but one way to find out. He shut the book and reached for the penknife in his desk drawer. He extended the blade and made an incision on the tip of his thumb, letting the blood drip onto the book.

On an especially warm spring evening, under the brilliant light of a full moon, William resolved to walk home after leaving his club. He had met a French psychologist at dinner, a guest visiting one of his colleagues at the hospital, who spoke about his adoption of moral therapy at his private asylum in Paris. The discussion left quite an impression on William, and he wandered the streets deep in thought.

Not paying particular attention as to where he was going, he cursed under his breath as he gave his ankle a turn on a protruding cobble stone. Limping cautiously forward a few steps, he was reassured that he had not injured it, and that he could make it back home without difficulty. He looked around as it suddenly dawned on him that he had strayed from the main road and was standing in one of the less reputable parts of town.

Good Lord, I'm nowhere near my home. I must have wandered about for a good hour to find myself in this part of town, which is definitely not where I want to be at such a late hour.

He oriented himself before taking a few steps forward only to come to an abrupt stop. About fifty paces in front of him, he saw a man exiting from what was surely a place of ill repute. William quietly stepped into the shadows and looked at the figure carefully.

Hello, is that who I think it is? Can it be James?

He followed the man until he had made his way to a more reputable part of the neighbourhood.

"James" he called out when he was a few paces behind.

The man turned with a start.

"James—I thought it was you," William said in surprise as he approached. His voice quickly changed to one of concern as he added, "My dear fellow, you look incredibly pale. Are you not well?"

"I have been...under the weather," he stammered, and then added quickly; "But my doctor assures me that I am on the mend. I have taken to strolling about in the evenings, as it helps me sleep more soundly. But what brings you out at this time of night?"

"I dined at my club tonight. It was such a beautiful evening that I decided to take a stroll before heading home." Making no mention of where he first spotted James, he continued, "I turned the corner at the base of the hill and there you were walking a short distance ahead of me. But why not accompany me to my residence for a glass of Brandy? It looks like it may do you well."

"No, no, thank you for the offer but I best make my way home."

There was an awkward pause before James added; "I have finished translating the text. I would like to show it to you in a few weeks time. There are certain...tasks I must complete first. I will send you notice when the time comes."

"I'll make sure to watch for it."

James tipped his hat then turned and hurried up the street.

Not at all like James, William thought, *what the devil is the man up to?*

The note arrived a month later. It read simply; *William—Please join me at my residence tomorrow at 5 p.m.* William was punctual the next day, and James welcomed him with his enthusiasm of old.

"So glad you could make it, my friend."

"It is always a pleasure to see you, James. I must say, you are looking much better than when I saw you last. I'm relieved to see you so full of vigor once again."

"Thank you, William. I am excited as I have something very important to show you. It is a thirty-minute ride from here. Please do not ask me what it is. I will explain everything once we get there. Let us go now, we can take my chaise."

They arrived at the ruins of a small castle as the sky turned overcast and a cool wind started to blow. James secured the horse reins to the bough of a stunted oak before motioning for William to follow him.

"I came here often as a child. My family would picnic on the grounds enclosed by the remains of the old tower walls. I would spend my time exploring the area. I found a tunnel entrance I never told my parents about. In fact, you are now the only other person who knows about it. Follow me down this steep embankment but watch your footing. As you can see, it is overgrown with shrubs and trees and the exposed roots can make it quite tricky to navigate down safely.

Once they had made their way down, William paused to catch his breath before speaking; "I am ill dressed for such an excursion. You should have advised me that we would be trekking down such rough terrain."

James pointed to his left and replied; "We are almost there. The entrance is about thirty yards in that direction. It is concealed by dense shrubs, quite impossible to find unless you were a restless ten-year-old boy who poked around every part of this place with a stick in hand throughout the summer."

With a smile, William said, "I'm anxious to see this secret entrance of yours. Please, lead the way."

The entrance was indeed well camouflaged, and punching their way through the thick entanglement of scrub was no easy task. Once they made their way to the mouth of the tunnel, James struck a match and lit a candle he had placed there on a previous occasion. An old door, made of heavy oak and reinforced with iron strips studded with large rivets, blocked the way forward.

Passing the candle to William, James said; "I've added a padlock to the door, hold the candle near so that I can insert the key and unlock it." Once unlocked, James hung the padlock on a hook by the door and slipped the key in his pocket. He took the candle from William and lead the way in, saying;

"We will be entering a chamber shortly. At one time there were probably steps that lead from the chamber directly into the interior of the castle, but they have long since been buried by rubble."

William could see little of the chamber by the light of the candle, so trailed closely behind James until they reached a small table, where James rested the candle next to a book.

"Good Lord, is that the book? The binding has been removed. What possessed you to do such as thing?" exclaimed William.

"Ah yes, the cover. I will get to that shortly," James replied. "But let me assure you the book is not damaged. You were correct in your surmise, William, in that the binding was of human skin, and it will be bound with it once more...albeit from that of a different person."

A heavy silence fell over the chamber before William spoke in a strained voice; "I think you should explain yourself, James."

"Without question I will. It is important that you, a man of science, understand what I am doing. This is incredibly exciting work I've embarked upon. But I'm getting ahead of myself. Let me start at the beginning." Pausing to gather his thoughts, he continued;

"Shortly after discovering the book, a few drops of blood fell upon it, the result of a minor nosebleed I experienced. When I went to wipe the cover clean, the blood was gone, and the binding itself seemed to have taken on a slight reddish undertone, as if it had *absorbed* the blood.

"This is, in fact, what had happened. As you suspected, the book delves into various elements of what you called 'dark magic', the most fascinating being the key to everlasting life. The skin that bound the book was from the alchemist Zacharie the Elder. Like many before him, he was attempting to create an elixir of immortality, and in one sense he succeeded, in that he found a method of transferring his life's essence, including all the knowledge he had accumulated during his lifetime, onto another person."

"Come now, James, this is utter nonsense!" cried William. "I believe you yourself described such books as 'superstitious rot', did you not?"

"I was wrong," James replied simply.

A candelabrum was placed near the edge of the table, and James used the candle's flame to light its four larger candles. Taking the candelabrum, he motioned for Williams to follow him. They walked a dozen paces towards the opposite wall.

The sight of what hung in front of them gave William a nasty turn, a sense of revulsion that made him feel sick to his stomach.

Two large spikes were driven into the chamber wall, about six feet above the ground and eight feet apart. A wire was threaded between the two spikes. Hanging from the wire, by a series of hooks, was a large, thin sheet. It was of a deep red hue, and its base rested in a shallow trough filled with a crimson liquid.

"My God," exclaimed William in a trembling voice, "can this be what I think it is?"

"It is, William. It is the original skin that bound the book, that of Zacharie the Elder. It has been nourished with blood—*human blood.* At first I used my own, but I could not provide enough to sustain its rapid growth. I was bleeding myself daily, which is why you observed me in such a poor condition on that evening one month ago. So I decided to seek another source.

"The thought occurred to me that a certain class of individuals might be willing to sell their blood. And so I wandered the more unsavoury parts of town in the evenings, until I found a brothel that would, for a profit, pay its girls and any willing customers for their blood. I conducted the bloodletting several times a week, and by this means I acquired the blood needed to nourish the skin's growth to the extent you see before you."

"What is it...you want from me?" asked William apprehensively.

"When the time comes for me to depart this world, provided I do not discover the elixir of immortality before then, I want you to remove a swath of skin from my body and have it made into the binding for the book, so that my life essence and wisdom are transferred to the future guardian of the book. You are a good ten years younger than myself, so I have little doubt you will outlive me and be able to fulfill this task."

"I beg of you James," William said earnestly, "destroy the book and do not proceed any further with this abomination. Immortality is not for us mortals. Death is our destiny."

James walked up to William and handed him the candelabrum. "I cannot. As to my original ask, I do not expect an answer from you now. If what you are about to witness does not convince you that I am telling the truth, then you are free to refuse my request. But I do not think you will."

James walked over and stood in front of the bloody tapestry, removed his clothes, and stepped into the trough of blood. He unhooked the skin and draped it over his head and body, turning to face William as he did so.

The man has gone too far, William cried under his breath, *his appearance is like that of a demon from hell. So much blood...*

Suddenly, the skin tightened itself around James, its blood oozing into his body as it did so. William could hear James gasping for breath as it tightened against his face, then came the sickening sound of flesh tearing as his nose and mouth tore through. He took in deep breaths as he looked about with a wild expression. Slowly his breathing steadied, and then, with a violent abruptness, he started to laugh out loud.

"I have done it, William! So much knowledge, I can barely keep track of the thoughts racing through my mind. What a feeling of absolute power. I sense the key to eternal life is within reach—I will discover it. I must! Join me in this quest, my dear friend. Together we can accomplish so much more..."

William remained silent, feeling a sudden wave of horror wash over him as he fixed his gaze on James. Patches of hair had fallen from Jame's head, and lesions were forming on his blood-streaked body.

Abruptly, James clutched his head with both hands and cried; "My head...such excruciating pain!" He bent down in agony and collapsed to his knees. Wart-like protrusions appeared on his torso and spread rapidly across the rest of his body. He fell over, his body shivering and twitching as he lay sprawled on the blood-soaked ground. He pleaded in a voice full of pain and despair; "Dear God, I cannot bear the pain any longer. William, help me, please! For the love of God, help...me..."

But there was nothing William could do. As a physician, he recognized the symptoms all too well, that of syphilis and typhoid, diseases that were sure to be present in the blood James collected from the prostitutes and their clients. James had used contaminated blood to feed the rapid growth of the severed skin, the same blood that now surged through his entire body, fueling the onset of such dreadful symptoms at an ungodly rate.

He knelt next to James' corrupted body, and with deep sorrow, uttered; "I'm so sorry, James, but there is nothing I can do. I hope Death will come and free you soon from such suffering.

May God have mercy on your soul when he does so."

William set the book ablaze before leaving the chamber. Once outside, he secured the padlock to the great wooden door with trembling hands, inclined his head slowly and leaned his forehead on the door as he whispered; "The key remains with you, my old friend. May no one ever come upon the horror that remains within."

The rain was falling heavily, but William took no notice as he made his way back to the chaise, his cheeks wet with tears.

THE HUNTER

Northern India, 1936

"Thank you for seeing me at such a late hour, Major O'Neal."

"I don't understand why this couldn't wait until the morning, inspector. However, I'm as keen as you are to put this dreadful matter to rest. It's the least I can do for poor Mary. Please come in. Can I offer you a drink?"

"No thank you, but I'd like to offer you one." Inspector Sahgal held up a bottle of Rum. "I'm officially off duty," he pointed out, winking.

"That's decent of you, inspector. Have a seat by the front window, there's a slight breeze this evening. I'll be with you in a minute."

The major returned with two glasses and took a seat across from the inspector. It was Inspector Sahgal who poured the drinks, then sat back and watched as the major downed his drink in one swift motion.

"I'm anxious to close the case of your wife's death," began the inspector as he refilled the major's glass, "so I'd like to go through the events of that day one more time. I know you gave a full statement a month ago, but there's one or two points that need clarification."

The major leaned back in his chair and lit a cigarette. "I'll do my best to answer your questions, inspector."

"Thank you, major," The inspector removed a well-worn notepad from his jacket pocket and thumbed through it until he came to a marked page, taking a moment to skim its contents. "I'm well aware of your international reputation as a big game hunter, but it is only recently that you decided to become a professional safari guide. Is that correct?"

"Yes, I'm getting on in years, and it seemed the wise thing to do."

"And your wife joined you as a guide?"

"On occasion. Mary was a good shot and acted as a guide whenever a husband was joined by his wife on the safari."

"I see," murmured the inspector, flipping to the next page of his notebook.

"Last month, on September twenty-second, you, along with your wife Mary and experienced assistant Aditya, left early that day to go on an expedition, is that correct?"

"It is not," the major replied. "It wasn't an expedition, inspector. We were to act as a guide for Sir Henry and Lady Grace later that week. They were interested in hunting tigers, so we decided to do a bit of scouting beforehand. We planned to be gone for no more than a couple of days."

"And this was typical—the scouting beforehand, I mean."

"Absolutely," replied the major decisively. "We went in search of any recent tracks to determine the level of difficulty posed by the terrain we would be hunting in. Forethought and careful planning are critical when hunting such cunning beasts."

The inspector agreed with a nod and then said; "It's important you walk me through the events of that day, major. From when you left that morning until your wife's unfortunate accident."

Major O'Neal rubbed his eyes and stifled a yawn before answering. "Forgive me, inspector, it's been a long day and I'm feeling rather tired all of a sudden. But I'll do my best to give you an accurate account."

"Thank you, major. I assure you I won't keep you much longer." The inspector refilled the major's glass.

The day began like any other," the major said, pausing to drink from his glass, "The gear had been packed the evening before so we set out soon after breakfast, around nine that morning. We found a set of tracks after an hour's hike. They lead northward, deeper into the jungle. Mary was feeling a bit off, so we pitched a small tent near a rock face so she could rest while Aditya and I followed the tracks further into the jungle."

"Was that wise, given the presence of a tiger nearby?"

"Naturally she had her Mauser rifle with her. You see, inspector, the tiger we were tracking was not the one that attacked Mary. It was probably a good ten miles from our location. The tiger that attacked Mary was a man-eater."

"A man-eater?" repeated the inspector in surprise. "Didn't that make the situation all the more dangerous? Why leave your wife there if you knew such a beast was in the area?"

"But we didn't know. It so happened that there was a tiger stalking a nearby village, having recently killed two of its members. Had we been informed of this by the authorities, we would have never gone out that day. But they failed to do so. As such, Aditya and I set off believing Mary was in no real danger."

"And you were gone for three hours?" asked the inspector, looking up from his notes.

"That's correct. When we got back, we saw the tent was in tatters. There was a trail of blood leading away from the area, and Mary's gun was found among the shredded fabric. It had not been fired. It was obvious the man-eater had detected her scent and pounced on the tent when Mary was inside. I found what remained of her body an hour later, about a mile from our site."

"You said 'I'. Why wasn't Aditya with you?"

"Now that was a curious affair," replied the major, stifling another yawn. "Aditya started babbling some nonsense about this being all his fault. I couldn't catch all he was saying as he intermixed Hindi with his English. As far as I was concerned, the man cracked, couldn't handle his guilt. He ran off like a madman and I haven't seen him since. In the state he was in I wouldn't be surprised if he fell pray to a lion or tiger that same day."

"But I understand he was a very experienced assistant, having gone on numerous hunting expeditions with some legendary hunters, yourself included. Why would he act in such an irrational manner, putting his life in danger?"

"Every man has his breaking point, inspector. I presume he reached his. What other reason can there be?"

The inspector did not respond but watched as the major struggled to keep his eyes open. He leaned back in his chair and shut his eyes. "Inspector," the major began, his speech slightly slurred, "I'm afraid I'll have to leave you now so I can get...some rest. Please see yourself—" His head suddenly slumped back, and he began to snore softly.

"My aching head," muttered the major as he rose slowly from the hard floor and looked around the small interior. The concrete room was six feet in both width and length, with one wall and its door constructed of metal bars. For a few short moments he thought he was imprisoned in a jail cell, but the view through the metal bars convinced him otherwise. The jungle lay a mere thirty feet away.

A few objects were visible by the entrance. "What the devil is going on here?" he asked himself, approaching the door. A canteen lay next to a double-barreled 12 bore shotgun, which he recognized as his own. Sitting atop the stock of the rifle was a letter addressed to Major O'Neal.

As the pain in his head began to subside, a feeling of unease overtook him as he stared down at the envelope. The events of the previous evening ran through his mind. *That blasted detective obviously laced my drink with a sedative. What's his game kidnapping a man of my caliber?* Reluctantly, he reached down and took the letter. It read as follows;

Major O'Neal—*I strongly advise you to read this letter in its entirety, as I am offering you a sporting chance of leaving this enclosure and returning to your residence alive, which is more than you offered poor Aditya and your wife. You see major, I know you murdered them both. In case you think I am bluffing, let me give you the details.*

After convincing your wife to come with you on the scouting expedition, you poisoned her the following morning at breakfast. You knew she would feel too ill to carry on after an hour's hike, so you had Aditya set up a tent for her, then sent him on ahead. You told him you would join him after you helped your wife get comfortable. She was probably unconscious shortly thereafter. You were well aware that a man-eater was prowling in the area, as several locals informed me that they had come and reported the incident to you just hours after the first killing. In your rucksack you had a jar with animal blood that you sprinkled on the outside of the tent. I know this because I had our lab conduct a precipitin test on the tent fabric confirming it was not your wife's blood as originally believed, but animal blood. Once you left her to join Aditya, your wife's fate was sealed. The odds were heavily in your favour that the man-eater or other tigers in the area would pickup the scent of fresh blood and feast on her body. As for Aditya, you shot him when you were well away from the tent. You couldn't take the chance that he'd contradict your version of events. I found his skeletal remains scattered in a gully. A large caliber bullet had shattered his skull.

Had you only done away with your wife, you would not have found yourself in this unique situation. I would still have suspected you of murder, after all, it was common knowledge that your gambling debts were getting out of control, and that your wife was not willing to share her substantial inheritance with you. And so you killed her for her money. A scenario I've seen played out many times during my career, and regrettably, one in which the husband is usually acquitted of the crime, as would be the case for a pukka sahib like yourself.

But you killed Aditya as well, who I swore to protect.

Fifteen years ago, you may recall that a tiger terrorized the people living on the outskirts of Bageshwar district by killing two children in as many days. I joined a hunting expedition to track down the man-eater. Aditya's father, Dheeraj, had also volunteered. We pursued a set of tracks heading north. The other hunters tracked a set of footprints along a riverbank close to the district.

That evening, we tried baiting the tiger with the carcass of a mongoose whose throat we had slit, but the beast did not make an appearance. We decided to head back the following morning and dug a shallow hole to rid ourselves of the carcass. I was a fool not to notice the droplets of blood that splattered onto my boots as I kicked the animal into its grave.

To make matters worse, we journeyed against the wind on our return to Bageshwar. The man-eater had no trouble catching our scent. Dheeraj was a mere ten paces behind me when the tiger pounced. By the time I turned and fired at the beast, Dheeraj was already fatally wounded . After I returned to Bageshwar I learned that one of the two children the man-eater had previously killed was his, and that his other boy was now an orphan. I felt it my duty to adopt the child. When he got older and I recounted what had happened to his father, Aditya swore he would become a great hunter one day. I believe he would have done so, had you not killed him.

I leave you with a canteen of water and your double barrel shotgun—with only one bullet in its chamber. The outskirts of Bageshwar is twenty miles eastward of your current location. If you make it back, you have my word that I will not proceed with your prosecution, as I have officially closed the case. The only obstacle standing between you and your freedom is a tiger.

The major looked up and stared at the jungle beyond as he recalled the events of that fateful day. "The inspector is no fool," he told himself. "He's figured things out well enough. But why play this absurd game with me? The death of Aditya must have unhinged the man."

Tearing the letter up, he tossed the pieces through the bars, watching as the wind carried them towards the jungle. He took up the canteen and poured some of its water into his cupped hand, bringing it close to his nose. *No odour. Still, I wouldn't put it past the man to try and poison me. I can go a couple of days without water.* He let the canteen fall to the ground then kicked it aside before reaching for his rifle. There was a single cartridge in one of the chambers, just as the letter had stated. He locked the barrel back into place and used the muzzle to nudge the cage door. It swung halfway open on its rusty hinges. He took a step forward and stood there for several minutes, listening, watching for any movement among the thick foliage of the jungle.

His experienced eye caught the faint rustling of leaves on a bush. A moment later a tiger emerged, raising its formidable head to sniff the air before turning its gaze towards the major. The beast didn't charge, but kept its eyes fixed in his direction, as if waiting for something to happen. Ever so slowly, the major lifted his gun and aimed it directly at the tiger's head. His finger was on the trigger when he heard a low growl over his shoulder. The major leaped back into the enclosure just as a second, larger tiger sprang from the roof, narrowly escaping the beast's lethal claws.

An hour passed and the major remained standing by the door, his nerves on edge due to a strange feeling of expectancy. The two tigers were lying under the shade of the jungle's canopy, twenty feet distance from each other. Both kept their focus on the major.

A Wolf snake slithered part way through the barred door before the major kicked it back out. It was then that he noticed the faded letters stamped on the concrete floor;

Property of Bageshwar Tiger Reserve

The hopelessness of his situation slowly dawned on him. "So, you have surrounded me with tigers," he said aloud. "I must admit, inspector, you are a clever devil. You would have made a worthy opponent as a tiger—"

His mind suddenly recalled the last phrase of the letter, '*The only obstacle standing between you and your freedom is a tiger.*' The major let out an ironic chuckle as he now understood its meaning. "So, inspector, you are that tiger. Well done! I see that you leave me no choice but to admit defeat...a single bullet will not get me very far in a tiger reserve...I will have to achieve my freedom another way."

He turned the barrel of the shotgun towards his head and pulled the trigger.

THE ASH MEN

West Texas, 1971

The five teenagers stood alone at the head of a dirt road that led to an old farmhouse about thirty feet away.

"So, what do ya think? Chad asked, giving Mark a slight shove on the shoulder, "Creepy enough for you?"

Mark didn't answer but looked over at Jessica, who had just snapped a photo of the old farmhouse.

"Gives me the creeps," she replied.

"Same here," Mark agreed. "Sure as hell wouldn't want to live there."

"Damn straight you wouldn't," replied Chad. "The place is haunted. Only a quack like Jenkins would live out here on his own. The mailman was just telling my mom that Jenkins hasn't collected his mail lately. Said maybe someone should go and check-in on him, see if—"

Mark stopped him short. "Why do they say it's haunted?"

"You need to ask?" Chad said in disbelief. "Just look at the place. No sign of life any-where, not even a bird chirping. Notice how the windows are barred, and there's that weird hex symbol painted over the doorway in red—maybe it's blood. You got to be blind not to recognize this place as haunted."

Mark stared at the house for a few moments, then looked over at Jessica once again. She nodded, so he turned his attention back to Chad and spoke;

"Alright Chad, you win this year's award for finding the creepiest house in Lukefalls this

Halloween. Jess and I will write-up a column in next week's school paper about this place. We'll also need a photo of you accepting the prize from Mrs. Johnson."

Matt and Johnny, who had remained silent up to this point, congratulated Chad with a firm slap on the back, saying; "Way to go, man," and "Chad always delivers the goods."

Mark glanced at Jessica and caught her rolling her eyes. He smiled slightly as he thought, *I know exactly what she's thinking—nothing but a macho band of troublemakers. She's right of course, but Chad did deliver on his promise, creepiest house I ever saw. Kids at school are going to come out here in droves.*

"You know what," Chad said as he took a step closer to Mark, "we can do one better. Everyone's gonna want to see the inside of the place. So why don't we show them?"

"Are you nuts? That's breaking and entering. We could be arrested, or worse, Jenkins could shoot us!"

"Get real. I'm talking about knocking on the door and straight-out asking him if we can photograph the place. Even if he says 'no', you'd probably be able to sneak a photo or two as he stands in the open doorway. Besides..." he added after a moment's reflection, "what if something has happened to the guy? The post-man did say someone should check in on Jenk-ins."

The group remained silent as Mark thought this over. It was Jessica who spoke first.

"He's right, you know. We should see if the guy's alright."

Mark shrugged and said hesitantly; "I guess so," but thought to himself, *When did Chad ever care about anyone?*

Three steps led up to the weathered wooden porch. Its railing had long since rotted away, leaving just the tall corner posts to support the low sloping roof. The floorboards creaked loudly as Chad, Mark and Jessica made their way to the door.

Chad took a quick breath and said, "Alright, here goes." Looking over at Jessica, he added; "Have your camera ready."

He gave three hard raps on the door and then stepped back slightly, motioning with his head for Jessica to move closer to the entrance. No one answered, not even after the second and third attempts.

Chad raised his eyebrows and wondered out loud; "Jeez, you don't think something really has happened to the guy?"

"Could be," Mark said. Then, looking at the door more closely, asked; "Why would anyone bolt the *outside* of their door?"

"Now that is weird," Chad agreed. He reached up and shot the bolt back. The door slowly swung half-way open into the entrance.

Jessica moved close to Mark and slid her hand under his arm. "I don't like this," she whispered.

"Neither do I," Mark replied under his breath.

Chad pushed the door fully open. "Mr. Jenkins," he called out loudly, "are you here? The postman asked us to check in on you." There was no response. He turned and motioned for

Matt and Johnny to join the others on the porch.

Matt shook his head. "Uh-uh, we're staying put."

"Yeah," added Johnny, "We're not leaving our bikes out here with no one to watch over them. You guys go ahead and look around inside if you want."

"Whatever," Chad scoffed, before turning to Matt and Jessica. "Let's have a quick look around. Jess, you can take a few photos while we're at it. Maybe the guy just decided to go on vacation."

The house was sparsely furnished, and the air was warm and stuffy, tinged with a slight acrid smell, as though there were traces of ash in the air. A column of floating dust particles was visible in the faint sunlight entering through the grated window of the entrance.

"He must really be afraid of someone breaking in," murmured Mark.

"Or breaking out..." added Chad in a lowered voice.

"What do you mean by that?" asked Jessica sharply.

"Relax, Jess. I was just trying to freak you out a little."

They took a few steps into the narrow hallway. The staircase leading to the second floor was immediately on their left, with the entrance to the living room a short distance past the stairs, where they slowly made their way. There was a fireplace on the far wall, a row of framed photographs displayed on the mantel. An old rocking chair sat at an angle to the fireplace, and opposite it along the outer wall, a worn sofa was positioned with its back to a row of windows, a stack of old newspapers scattered on its cushions. Adjacent to this room was the dining room, furnished with a small, rectangular table and a cross-back chair at each end. One of the kitchen entrances led into the dining room, the other was located at the end of the entrance hallway.

"Cheery place, isn't it?" Chad said off-handedly as he looked about the room with its stained and barren walls. "I think I'll go check out the kitchen. If there's food rotting in the fridge then we'll know something's up."

Jessica began to snap a few photos as Mark made his way to the fireplace to have a look at the photographs. There was a half-dozen, seemingly placed in chronological order, with the first being a faded, black and white photo with the date 1852 scrawled on its lower corner. The image was of a man in his forties, of thin build and dressed in safari gear, standing next to a group of natives sitting behind a bed of smoldering coals, their bodies and faces covered in soot. Each of the other photos depicted a similar scene, with the last photo, taken with a Polaroid instant camera, dated 1969.

"Do you think the guy in the photo is Jenkins?" asked Jessica, as she approached Mark.

"Maybe," he replied absently while studying the image. He slid the box of matches that was next to the photograph to one side before he spoke again.

"Jess, do me a favour and bring me the first photo on the mantel."

She did so and he placed the photograph next to the Polaroid one.

"They sure look like the same guy," Jessica observed.

"Can't be...," replied Mark in a slow, puzzled voice. "Look at the dates on the photos. They were taken...let's see...one-hundred and...seventeen years apart."

"Well then, the photos must be of a father and his son."

Mark shook his head. "That makes no sense, Jess. Even if he became a father twenty years after the first photo was taken, his son would be ninety-seven years old, but the guy in the Polaroid is in his forties."

His thoughts were interrupted as Chad entered the dining room from the kitchen entrance and began heading towards the stairs. "Fridge is empty except for some meat in the freezer. There's also a door that leads down to the cellar. I took a quick look from the top of the stairs. The dim lighting made it hard to see, but it doesn't look like there's much down there. I'm going to check upstairs. I'll holler if I find the guy."

It's as if he's enjoying this, thought Mark, as he watched Chad take the steps two at a time.

Jessica took Mark's hand and lead him towards the entrance. "I need some air. I'm getting a little creeped out by this place."

Just then, Chad called out from the top landing. "Guys, come on up, I found Jenkins."

Mark and Jessica stared at each other in disbelief. Jessica said;

"I swear, if this is one of his pranks I'm going to kick the guy full force between the legs."

"Wouldn't mind seeing that," murmured Mark as they made their way up the stairs.

A single window at the end of the corridor illuminated the upstairs hallway. Three rooms, all lacking doors, were on the right side. The first was a small bathroom with nothing more than a wash basin, toilet and tub. The second room had no furniture, only dark stains on the wooden floor and walls. Chad could be found waiting by the doorway of the third room.

"In here," he said, stepping into the room.

Mark and Jessica cautiously made their way forward. Chad stood in front of a double bed, with its sheet and blankets strewn about. Next to the bed, there was a small night table and lamp.

Chad nodded towards the corner of the room behind them. "Over there," he said.

"Jesus!" exclaimed Mark as he turned and spotted the body sitting on the floor, its back propped up against the corner, the head slumped forward. He stumbled back a few steps with Jessica right beside him, gripping his arm tightly.

"Is he...is he...dead?" Jessica stammered.

"Sure looks like it," answered Chad. "Must have passed away recently as I don't smell anything rotting."

"Is it Jenkins?" Mark asked.

Chad shrugged his shoulders. "Who else can it be? It's got to be him."

Mark studied the body from where he was standing. It was clad in worn-out denim overalls and was barefoot. Its arms hung limply by its side, grimy and coated in a fine layer of soot, as though it had been labouring away in a coal mine.

Same build and reddish hair colour as the guy in the photos downstairs, Mark thought. *But there's no way I'm getting any closer to check out his face.*

"Tell you what," began Chad, "Why don't you guys go downstairs and tell Matt and Johnny to hop on their bikes and head to a neighbour's house to call an ambulance. I'll meet you downstairs after I use the washroom. Nature's calling badly."

As they approached the bottom of the stairs, Jessica asked uneasily, "Why's the door shut?"

Mark remained silent as he went up to it and gave the handle a hard pull. The door didn't budge.

"Hey, assholes!" he burst out as he pounded his fist against the door. "Unbolt the door. Jenkins is dead. We need an ambulance!"

He waited for a minute but there was no re-ply. Frustrated, he made his way to the living room and leaned over the sofa to peer out the front window. He saw no one, and then slowly felt a knot tighten in his gut when he noticed the bikes were missing.

"Shit, this is not good," he murmured.

As he pushed off from the windowsill and straightened up, one of the newspapers on the sofa caught his attention, a 1905 edition of The New York Times, its headline stark against the yellowed paper; *Disappearance of Jenkins' Expedition Continues to Mystify After Half a Century.* The picture below the headline was the same as the one on the mantelpiece dated 1852.

"Jess, come see this."

Mark was engrossed in the article when Jessica walked into the room. She came up beside him and read the headline.

"What happened?" she asked, a tinge of nervousness in her voice.

"Apparently," began Mark, "Jenkins led one of the first expeditions to be funded by the American Geographic Society. He was to explore the Congo Basin, but he never made it back to America. Listen to this;"

The local guides, by way of an interpreter, informed the society that deep within the Congo Basin the expedition team encountered an ancient tribe know as 'The Ash Men'. The guides, who greatly feared the tribe, urged Jenkins and his men to abandon their quest. They refused, and so the guides left them and returned home. When asked why they feared the tribe, they told the following gruesome account;

The Ash Men are purported to be cannibals who mix the blood of their victims with the ash from their burnt remains. As a final step before ingesting the concoction, they cover their bodies with the victim's ashes, performing a dark and ancient ritual as they finally consume the mixture. As nothing can destroy ash, so the Ash Men themselves cannot be destroyed. They can live on for hundreds of years, provided they repeat the sacred ritual every twenty years.

Mark dropped the newspaper and looked over at the mantelpiece.

"Six photos," he said, "each dating twenty years apart, the first taken in 1852 and the most recent in 1969. In every photo he's standing next to the Ash Men, never looking older. He became one of them."

"I'm scared Mark.," Jessica uttered gravely.

"So am I," Mark admitted. "But he's dead now. Let's go get Chad and find a way out of here. I've had all I can take of this place. I'm sure the three of us together can get the front door open."

They made their way up the stairs, calling Chad's name when they reached the landing. There was no reply. *What's he playing at now?* Mark murmured uneasily.

"Hey Chad, quit playing around, we need to get out of here."

They walked uneasily towards the bedroom, stopping to glance in each room as they did so. From the bedroom doorway, everything looked as it did previously. Mark entered and fixed his gaze on the corner where Jenkins sat, and in a strained voice lined with fear uttered, "Jesus!"

It was not Jenkins' body seated in the corner, but that of Chad's, his throat slit, streaks of crimson running down the front of his white t-shirt.

Jessica entered and managed to stifle her scream as she looked on in horror.

"Where's...Jenkins?" she stammered.

Mark glanced around the room nervously. "I don't know. He's not in here and he wasn't in the other rooms when we passed by. Let's get out of here, Jess. Now."

They tried the front door several times but eventually gave up.

"It's no use," Mark said while catching his breath, looking around at the barred window and locked door. "This place is set up like a prison. Somehow, we need to find another way out." The faint noise of a floorboard creaking made Matt and Jessica pause. They lifted their gazes towards the ceiling. Shortly after, another creak was heard, followed by another. It was clear that someone, or something, was advancing towards the staircase.

"Head for the kitchen, Jess. We need to find something to defend ourselves with."

They frantically rummaged through the kitchen drawers. It was Jessica who found the grim collection of butcher knives. Mark handed her a razor-sharp boning knife from the pile.

"No way Mark. I can't."

"Take it, Jess!" he said forcefully, grabbing the large meat cleaver for himself. "The basement is our last hope. Basement windows are usually small, so he may not have barred them. Maybe we can squeeze our way through."

"And if we can't?"

He didn't answer, but his eyes narrowed on the knife in her hand.

She trembled slightly before nodding in comprehension, then turned and flipped the light switch at the top of the stairs. The lone light bulb at the base of the steps did not turn on.

"Just perfect," she said under her breath.

"Let's go Jess, I hear it coming down the stairs."

A musty odor of damp earth lingered in the air. Three small windows on the far wall at ground level let in the diminishing daylight, casting shadows across the basement. Mark's hunch had proven correct—the windows had no security bars.

"Hand me your knife Jess, and I'll give you a boost. Reach-up and open the latch. Watch your head as the window will swing forward."

She did as Matt said, but the window remained shut, so she tried pulling the latch forward with all her strength.

"Mark, why isn't it opening?" she said in desperation, banging her fist against the glass several times.

"Jess stop...stop!"

He let go of her and she dropped back down beside him.

"It's no good, Jess. They're bolted shut. I only noticed it when you were tugging at the latch."

"Then smash the glass!"

"I will. Stand back and I'll use the—"

He stopped short of finishing his sentence. Something came creeping down the stairway. Mark grabbed Jessica's arm and drew her beside him, returning the knife to her. His heart thumped madly as he raised the meat cleaver over his head, ready to strike.

In an instant, something pounced forward from the shadowy depths with a tremendous cry before erupting into hysterical laughter. It was Chad in his bloody t-shirt.

"You should see...your faces!" he managed to say between fits of laughter. "Matt...Johnny...you can come down now."

The two came down laughing, with Johnny remarking, "Oh man...you scared them shitless, just like you said you would!"

Mark and Jessica were left in stunned silence, trying to comprehend what had just happened. Suddenly, Jessica took a step forward and pointed her knife at Chad, her voice dripping with rage as she said "You moron! I ought to—"

"Full of courage now, aren't we?" Chad interrupted in a mocking tone.

Mark reached out and pulled Jessica back, asking Chad in bewilderment, "But how?"

"How? Me and the boys came here yesterday to check the place out for the contest. The front door was open, so we took a look around. Found Jenkins dead upstairs, just as you saw him. And then I had my brainstorm. Got the guys to add a deadbolt to the outside door so you couldn't leave the place. I hid some fake blood in the bedside table and everything was all set for the next day. I made it look like I just discovered Jenkins body, and when you guys went down to tell the boys to get an ambulance, I slid Jenkins under the bed, squirted the blood on my neck and t-shirt, and took his place in the corner. In the meantime, the boys had bolted the front door shut and hid their bikes. I waited for you to come back upstairs and get the shock of your life. Once you returned downstairs, I started my slow walk towards the stairs. The boys were hiding just below the entrance window. I knocked on the glass when I got to the bottom of the stairs to let them know it was safe to come in. Then I made my way to the cellar so that I could finish scaring the crap out of you."

"But why...what did we ever do to you?" Jessica asked, her voice still tinged with anger.

"Why?" repeated Chad in a defiant manner, "Because I hate your guts, the both of you. Mister and Misses perfect, teacher's pet, 'most likely to succeed'. Well now we can tell everyone what you're really made of— just a couple of gutless, whining, wimps. Everyone at school and all of Lukefalls will hear about it, I'll see to that. There's no place you can go without someone saying, 'there goes that wimp Mark and his pathetic girlfriend.'"

A feeling of unease crept over Mark. Something Chad had said about hiding Jenkins' body now struck him as odd. He asked suddenly;

"Was Jenkins' body stiff when you moved it?"

"Stiff? No way, you saw his limp body in the corner. I just pulled him by the arms when I slid him under the bed."

"That's not good...not good at all. A body goes stiff a few hours after death, but his wasn't. I'll bet you it didn't even feel cold. We're in a heap of trouble now, Chad. Jenkins is not dead."

"C'mon Mark, give it a break. You can't scare us. You got royally burned. Live with it."

"Listen to him, Chad," put in Jessica. "You don't know about Jenkins. He's one of the Ash Men, a freaking cannibal who can't die. He played you for the idiot you are. Now he's got five bodies trapped in the cellar to feast on."

The three of them gave a short laugh, but Jessica could detect a hint of fear in their eyes.

"You're full of it, Jess. Let's go get some dinner boys and leave these two to the cannibals—"

A low, bestial laugh emanated from under the stairwell.

Chad's face turned pale. "What are you playing at Mark?"

Mark didn't answer but tightened his grip on the meat cleaver.

Again, a sound came from beneath the steps. This time it was more guttural, the sound of something savage...something hungry.

Chad and his cronies turned and peered into the darkened corner. Mark motioned for Jessica to move as far away as she could from them. "Head for the stairs the first chance you get," he whispered.

With a great yell Jenkins sprang from the darkness, a savage, appalling look on his face. He was upon the three boys in an instant, driving a hatchet into Matt's skull and slitting Johnny's throat. Chad screamed as Jenkins bit into his neck, tearing away at it savagely.

Mark shouted, "Run Jess!"

She dropped the knife and fled, stumbling up the darkened stairwell. Mark was a few steps behind her when he was struck suddenly on the side of the face. He fell to his knees in a daze for a brief moment, then noticed the severed hand on the step ahead of him.

"C'mon Mark!" Jessica yelled from the top of the stairs.

He stumbled forward and was through the doorway when a hand grabbed his ankle. Mark fell hard, hitting his jaw on the kitchen floor. Jenkins leapt onto his back in an instant, pulling his head back forcefully by the hair. And then there was the sound of crushing bone as Jenkins released his grip and toppled over.

Dropping the heavy cast-iron pan, Jessica helped Mark to his feet. They were both trembling, trying to catch their breath as they looked over at Jenkins, whose face was now a bloody mess, his nose shattered into a pulp. Slowly, he turned his head to look at them, and then a faint smile crept over its face, followed by a low chuckle.

"Oh, shit!" Mark cried as he grabbed Jessica's hand and ran down the hall. By the living room entrance he said, "Wait for me by the door. Go!"

He grabbed the box of matches from the fireplace mantel and set the newspapers alight. The couch was in flames in a matter of seconds. Igniting the entire box of matches, he tossed it at the curtains. A column of flame and smoke leapt to the ceiling, setting the wooden planks ablaze.

Jessica was standing by the front doorway as he rushed out of the living room, her hand on the doorknob, waiting to slam it shut. He took one look at her anxious face and knew what stood at the end of the hallway.

"C'mon!" she yelled.

Mark ran, the maniacal laughter of Jenkins close behind. He dove through the doorway as Jessica slammed it shut, his momentum carrying him down the porch steps.

"Mark! I can't hold the door much longer!"

Jessica was pulling on the door handle with booth hands, one foot raised and pushing against the door frame for leverage. He rushed to her side and grabbed the handle, yelling "the bolt—reach for the bolt."

"I can't. I'd have to let go of the handle."

"Do it Jess, now!"

She released her hold. The door creaked inwards slightly and Mark felt the handle slipping from his grip. And then came the sound of the bolt being slammed shut.

The two of them collapsed onto the porch, exhausted. The fire was raging now, the windows shattering from the tremendous heat. They made their way unsteadily down the steps, the insane laughter of Jenkins still echoing from within the blazing inferno.

Jessica and Mark stood together, leaning on each other, watching as the house started its inward collapse. Mark looked up and became aware of a small, dark haze that broke away from the billowing smoke clouds and started to drift southwards, against the prevailing wind.

"Jenkins," murmured Mark. "Nothing can destroy ash…"

"What's that?" asked Jessica.

"Nothing. Let's get out of here."

There was the faint sound of a siren in the distance as the two slowly made their way down the empty dirt road.

Excerpt From 'The Inheritance & Other Dark Tales'

The Inheritance (1831)

Richard Hartley, twenty-seven years of age, good-looking with light blue eyes and wavy brown hair, stood just inside the entrance gate, the shade of a large elm providing some relief from the heat of the midday sun. He was admiring the imposing facade of Elliot House, a stately manor surrounded by ten acres of land and bordered by dense woodland to the north and east. The estate was built upon a prominent hill at the outskirts of Easby village, and until recently, belonged to Sir Elliot, Richard's great uncle. Sir Elliot fell victim to a persistent cough after returning from a short excursion foxhunting in the vicinity of Barnard Castle and passed away of consumption several weeks later. As a childless widower, Sir Elliot had named Richard, his only surviving relative, as heir and executor of his estate.

Sir Elliot's solicitors, Henwood & Thomson, had communicated with Richard a fortnight ago, informing him of his uncle's demise and that Richard was the sole beneficiary of his last will and testament. Upon the news, Richard sold his few possessions, gave notice to his employer (he worked as a clerk at Sheffield and Hallamshire Bank) and hired a private chaise to transport him to Elliot House, as he could now afford such luxury. The distance was less than eighty miles, but the journey proved unexpectedly long. A severe thunderstorm hampered the journey early on, and an outbreak of equine influenza earlier that summer meant that the coaching inns had no horses to let for the subsequent stages of Richard's journey. The entire trip had to be completed by the original pair of horses, necessitating frequent and prolonged stops so that the animals could feed and rest. Richard had planned to arrive at Elliot House on Saturday morning, but it was not until noon of the following day that the chaise drew up to the front gate, leaving Richard at the spot where he now stood.

Reaching for the suitcase by his side, he proceeded, somewhat hesitantly, along the wide gravel path leading to the front entrance.

Steady on, he thought to himself. *This is all yours now, no need to be shy.*

He picked-up his pace, soon reaching the front steps which he took two at a time, managing not to knock the bottom of his heavy suitcase as he did so. He paused at the front entrance to catch his breath, then removed the latch key provided by Henwood & Thomson from the bill compartment of his wallet. He tapped the key a few times on his palm while studying the door—a solid oak, six-panel affair bordered on each side by white columns, across the top of which ran a classically en-graved frieze.

"Well Richard," he said pensively to himself, "a new life awaits you beyond this door. A life of leisure and, let us hope, much happiness. I guess it would be appropriate to say a few words of thanks to Sir Elliot before entering." He was silent for a moment, then said:

"Thank you kindly uncle...I will be forever grateful..."

Not knowing what more to say, he looked down at his feet while stroking his chin for a minute, then lifted his head and with a slight shrug of his shoulders added:

"Forgive me uncle, I'm not very good with speeches, but know that I am truly thankful..." Pausing to reflect once more on his own life, Richard went on, "I presume the servants will address me as 'Master Richard'—I can hear my manservant now, greeting me with 'I under-stand Master Richard was a most accomplished bank clerk in Sheffield...'" He chuckled at this before continuing, "Doesn't quite compare to uncle's adventurous life, making his fortune in India as an exporter of raw goods. Well, not something I have to concern myself with today, as there are no servants about—I'm sure they are happy enough to have the weekend off. I'm certainly glad they are not here—it grants me the time to explore the house on my own." At this point he gently shook his head disapprovingly and said, "But come now Richard, this will never do—enough of this idle chatter, it's time to enter your house."

The entrance hall was elegantly but sparsely decorated, as were many of the other rooms in the house. The second floor had six bedrooms, including a very large master suite which Richard believed to be the size of his previous flat (no doubt an exaggeration on Richard's part). On the ground floor was the kitchen, sitting room, conservatory, dinning and drawing rooms, as well as the study.

Now this is interesting, thought Richard as he stepped into the study. The character of the room was in keeping with the general decor of the house—Wedgwood blue walls with a few large portraits in gilded frames. A mahogany, leather-top desk faced two large windows, and waist-high barrister bookcases lined one wall.

It was the incongruous item standing alone on the opposite wall that had caught Richard's attention—a large vitrine cabinet. The display unit rested on square tapered legs that ended in brass cloven feet. The woodwork was accented with a finely carved, ophidian design, and two glass doors enclosed four shelves against a mirrored back. The shelves themselves were filled with an odd assortment of strange and exotic objects.

"Why, this is a curio cabinet," said Richard excitedly. "I had no idea uncle was such an avid collector."

Swinging the doors open, Richard proceeded to examine the items, each of which was identified by a neatly scripted museum label, each describing the object. A shrunken head on the bottom shelf was the first item to catch his attention.

"Ghastly object," he said, removing it from the shelf gingerly. He reached for its label and read, "Head of Captain Antonio de Herrera, Shipwrecked, Ecuador Expedition, 1699."

So, such things really do exist, he thought, *I was skeptical when Charles told me about them years ago—he was always telling tall tales to his class-mates. If I remember his gruesome account correctly, the flesh is peeled back from the skull, then the bones and brain are removed and replaced with sand as the skin is stitched back together. What a frightful way to end one's life. May his soul rest in peace.* He carefully returned the head to its spot. Next to it was a pair of Hindu fakir's sandals. They were studded with dozens of rusty iron spikes that projected up through the soles. Richard tapped the spikes cautiously with his forefinger. *They really are quite sharp—amazing how these fakirs were able to conquer physical pain.*

Other items Richard examined included a preserved specimen in a jar that looked like a monstrous worm, at least three feet in length, an Egyptian mummified cat, and a clockwork automaton of a singing bird in a lovely gilded cage, its tune and head movements extremely lifelike. He had just started to shut the cabinet doors when he spotted a section of a skull on the far corner of the top shelf.

What do we have here? The bone was from the front of a skull, the portion surrounding the ocular sockets and nasal cavity. *Resembles a mask one would wear to a masquerade ball—far more gruesome, of course. Let's see what the label tells us.* The label was in a different penmanship than the others, and simply read: 'See through the eyes of a witch.'

Richard gave a short laugh upon reading this and exclaimed, "Oh come now uncle, this really is going too far!"

He took the bone mask off the shelf, turned towards the window and held it at arm's length, aligned with his sightline. The view through the eye sockets was blurred, he could not make out either the desk or windows that were but twenty feet in front. His first reaction was to thrust his finger through the eye holes to see if there was a lens present—there was not.

Queer, thought Richard, *must be a trick of the light.*

He repeated his action, but this time he brought the bone slowly towards his face.

How curious, the room is coming slowly into focus, as if I were adjusting the eyepiece on a spyglass...

Richard continued this movement until the skull came in contact with his own face.

Unbelievable, everything is so crisp and clear, superior to my own eyesight.

He was still holding the skull piece to his face when he felt a slight pressure against his forehead. His hands moved instinctively to remove the bone mask, but they came away empty. The mask remained attached to his face. There was a tightening in his throat as panic slowly overtook him—the pressure of the bone against his face was beginning to increase. He turned towards the cabinet and saw his reflection in the mirror. The bone mask was being absorbed into his face. He could feel and hear his own flesh sucking the bone in, folding over it as it sunk deeper into his flesh, driving the bone ever closer to his own skull. He let out an agonizing scream, falling to his knees as he clutched at his face. His head spun violently, and a moment later he collapsed.

A native of Ontario, Canada, Stephen intertwines his academic prowess with a lifelong passion for the paranormal. Growing up with tales of "true" ghost stories from his grandparents' séances and after-school sessions with "The Twilight Zone," Stephen has cultivated a deep-seated fascination for stories that delve into the horror and paranormal genres. Stephen brings a unique blend of scholarly insight and personal intrigue to his writing, creating tales that not only entertain but also resonate with a chilling touch of authenticity. A Tarot Prophesy and Other Stories is his third book.

ALSO BY STEPHEN TALLEVI

The Inheritance and Other Dark Tales

Indulge in a spine-tingling experience with this collection of haunting and macabre stories, perfect for horror enthusiasts. From mysterious Bone Gatherers that dwell deep within Europe's catacombs to ancient Pagan cults that harvest human eyes, this haunting collection is sure to keep you awake well into the early hours of the morning.

"The Inheritance and Other Dark Tales" is not for the faint of heart... a thrilling read for fans of horror"- *Readers' Favorite*

"A gripping collection of horror stories...a brilliant and unforgettable book." - *Literary Titan*

www.ingramcontent.com/pod-product-compliance
Lightning Source LLC
Chambersburg PA
CBHW020655120726
47906CB00001B/277